Heat began to penetrate her

Heat from Justin's body as he pulled her close and caught her mouth in a sweet, savage kiss. "Oh, *chère*," he murmured.

Part of Lucy knew this was wrong. That she should back off before they got caught up in something they couldn't stop. Something that might even get him killed.

But another part of her couldn't help herself. One kiss, Lucy thought. Just one sexy kiss.

Justin swept his hands over her breasts. Her nipples hardened and the soft flesh ached for more. His tongue plunged deep inside her mouth, the rhythm making her think of him plunging deep inside her.

A moment later he pulled her out of the chair and against his chest. She felt his throbbing length through her clothing. Hands cradling her bottom, he pressed his erection low against her belly. Oh, the sensations that spread through her like wildfire! Her hips began to move, and more than anything she wanted to rid them both of their garments.

She could just picture it. Naked. Her straddling him in the darkened bedroom.

She moaned and Justin swallowed the sound as if he were having the very same fantasy.

As if he'd had the very same dream…

Blaze™

Dear Reader,

What's hotter than a sultry Louisiana night? For my heroine
Lucy Ryan, nothing. Lucy has psychic dreams…psychic erotic
dreams of a man she doesn't know…yet. Justin Guidry comes
into her life just when she needs him to get her out of a jam.
Then, not only is her life at risk, but her heart, as well.

I had a great time writing Lucy and Justin's story. Almost as great
as I did exploring New Orleans itself. So pull up a comfy chair,
pour yourself a cup of chicory coffee, grab a beignet and enjoy
In Dreams.

Happy reading,

Patricia Rosemoor

Books by Patricia Rosemoor

HARLEQUIN BLAZE
35—SHEER PLEASURE*
55—IMPROPER CONDUCT*
95—HOT ZONE*

*Chicago Heat

IN DREAMS

Patricia Rosemoor

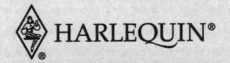

HARLEQUIN®

TORONTO • NEW YORK • LONDON
AMSTERDAM • PARIS • SYDNEY • HAMBURG
STOCKHOLM • ATHENS • TOKYO • MILAN • MADRID
PRAGUE • WARSAW • BUDAPEST • AUCKLAND

To Edward...see you in dreams...

ISBN 0-373-79155-0

IN DREAMS

Copyright © 2004 by Patricia Pinianski.

www.eHarlequin.com

Printed in U.S.A.

1

SHE SWEPT HER TONGUE up his hard length. His moan sent fingers of fire down her body to the heat between her thighs.

She wanted him there.

Slowly, she eased her body upward until their mouths met. He swallowed her whole with that kiss, making her feel as if she were drowning. Ending the kiss, she pushed herself up so she could see him. His sharp features, punctuated by a fall of inky hair across his high forehead, had never seemed so alive. Heavy lids over pale brown eyes revealed the promise of pleasure...bedroom eyes that could make her insides curl.

Her insides were curling now.

She felt him moving under her, his hot hands on her thighs, a clever thumb lingering at her sweet spot. He stroked her clit until she arched back and opened herself wider to him.

''Now, chère, *now,'' he urged.*

She wanted to hold on, to draw out the pleasure a while longer, but he wouldn't ease up on her and the friction push-push-pushed her over the edge. As the pulsing began deep inside her, she dug her nails into

*his thighs. He jerked and made a low guttural sound.
Then a treacherous sound pushed them both into the
abyss from which there was no rescue....*

"A-ah!"

Suddenly awake, Lucy Ryan sat straight up, her
body soft and humming with pleasure from the erotic
dream. But there was no pleasure in the pounding of
her heart, like that of a frightened bird captured in
flight.

In flight—that she was—and the erotic dream was
in reality a nightmare....

The image of her lover came back to her as clearly
as if he stood before her. Sharp features. Inky hair.
Bedroom eyes.

She didn't know anyone who looked like that.

At least not yet.

Dear Lord, no. She couldn't bring anyone else into
this, she couldn't risk another life. But even as she
denied it, Lucy knew she had no control over what
was shown to her in dreams.

A glance at the glowing numbers of the digital clock
told her it was barely four. She'd slept a little more
than an hour. Climbing off the thin mattress, she tried
to stop herself from shaking as she made her way into
the bathroom.

The motel was cheap and threadbare, but at least it
was clean. She washed her face, then stepped into the
shower, hoping the warm water would soothe her. Instead, it cleared her mind, made her remember too
sharply what she had witnessed several hours ago, a
nightmare turned real.

She couldn't stop the dreams from coming, couldn't change them. And because of that, a young woman was dead. And she was on the run, fleeing from the murderer's accomplices who were after her.

The only witness.

So what the hell was she supposed to do next?

Now that she had time to think, to consider her options, Lucy realized she had to go back to New Orleans and contact the police, tell them everything she knew. Rather, a version they could handle. That was the only way. Earlier she'd panicked and headed out of the city to anywhere away from the danger following her, but eventually she'd lost the thugs. And if she went back to the city how in the world would they know where to find her?

Reassured, she quickly pulled on her cotton flood pants and crop top, then shoved her feet into thick-soled sandals.

The authorities wouldn't believe her if she told them everything, but she didn't have to explain that she'd purposely gone to the scene of the crime, but had been too late to save that poor woman. She could simply say she'd been out for a walk and had stumbled on the murder. That would be believable. New Orleans was a late-night town and on weekends pedestrians crowded French Quarter streets.

In her mind's eye, Lucy could again see the horror she hadn't been able to stop. But before fear could change her mind, she shook away the memory.

Scraping a thick skein of coppery hair from her eyes, she grabbed her wallet and shoved it in her pocket—she'd left her shoulder bag on the floor of her car. Then she found her keys and peeked through the blinds. The motel sign glowed at her through a wet neon haze. There was no one was out to see her leave. Opening the door to a blast of humidity, she crossed the rain-slick pavement to her car.

It wasn't until she pulled out of the parking lot and checked her rearview mirror that she saw a set of high beams turn on.

Her chest tightened, but she told herself someone else had merely chosen to leave the motel at four in the morning. Though the rain had stopped and the moon was trying to pop out from behind a cloud, she turned on her wipers to clear the windshield, then checked the mirror again. The other car swung out behind her. Coincidence, she told herself, but just to make certain, she took a turn she hadn't meant to on a road she didn't know.

The other car followed.

She pressed the accelerator harder.

The other car kept pace.

She made another turn.

The other car turned, as well.

Her mouth was dry, her pulse fierce, but she told herself to stay calm. She was intelligent enough to think her way out of this.

Think!

They were speeding along a moonlit bayou, the long narrow finger of water crossed by home-built bridges to small dwellings, mostly ramshackle, some boarded up. Fishing camps probably, but none so far showed any sign of life. And there was no doubling back.

Her headlights hit a sign that indicated a split ahead. *Which way to go?*

Driving on instinct, she stayed left, venturing deeper into bayou territory, and when she saw another road ahead and to the right—this one gravel—she killed her lights and made a wild turn, trusting the moon to guide her.

A check of her rearview mirror revealed a flash of lights as the other car continued on past her.

Drawing a shaky breath, she took her foot off the accelerator and let the car slow. But her relief was short-lived. A beam of light swept over her from behind. Checking her mirror, she realized the other driver had turned around somewhere and was once more on her tail.

The moment of distraction proved disastrous. Her left wheels strayed off the gravel, and when she tried to steer the car back onto the road, she couldn't. The wheels spun, spitting gravel on one side, mud on the other. The car slipped and slid sideways and then started to tilt as if it were sinking. A cypress loomed before her and she slammed on the brakes just in time to avoid crashing into it.

Not stopping to count her blessings, Lucy cut the engine, and grabbed her car keys with its micro light attached to the key ring. Not that she would use the tiny light now, but it might come in handy later. Wincing as the mud sucked at her feet, trying to trap her, she pushed herself away from the road. She had al-

In Dreams

ways been a city girl, but thankfully she'd never been girlie-squeamish.

She glanced back. The other car had stopped.

"Don't run, *chère,* no place for you to go now!" a man called out as she slopped through ankle-deep swamp water.

Heart beating wildly, she plunged ahead. Two doors slammed and she assumed they were now after her on foot.

"We just want to talk to you," the second man singsonged. "Them alligators, they like a tasty meal."

"I'll take my chances," she breathed, knowing alligators killed to eat, not because they were trying to cover up a crime. *Talk?* Yeah, right.

Moonbeams filtered down through the cypress trees, giving her just enough illumination to find her way. Unfortunately, the light was undoubtedly enough for the two men to see her. She heard them splashing through the shallows in her direction. One of them cursed and the word *shoe* drifted to her.

If she weren't so afraid she might smile.

She tried to move soundlessly through the swamp.

Maybe she could lose them.

There was a splash to her left. Not the two men. Her throat tightened.

An alligator!

But she realized nature was the last thing she ought to be worrying about when one of the men said loudly, "Let's get this over with. Shoot the bitch!"

Glancing back, she saw one of the them raise his

arm and a dull blue glow suddenly flared into heat...
heat that tore at her side and made her stumble....

Shot!

Before she could grasp the concept, before she
could move to find a place to hide, a hand covered her
mouth and an arm snaked around her waist and
dragged her back into the shelter of a cypress.

His "Shhh" was unnecessary. She had no intention
of calling out so they could find her more easily.

But who was *he?* A definite he. No softness behind
her. Only hard muscle and a tension that was contagious. Almost enough to distract her from the pain
burning her side.

The shooter said, "I think I got her—"

"Dammit, I lost my other shoe!"

"Screw the shoe! Better than losing your life. Let's
go make sure."

"You wanna go, then you go. There's something
moving in that water."

"What? An alligator?"

"This is the swamp, idiot, whad'ya think? We can
come back to finish the job tomorrow when we can
see what's what."

She heard them cursing, then their voices receded.
They were moving back toward their car. Her knees
grew weak and she sagged back in relief.

Her rescuer waited a beat, then whispered, "I'm
going to let go, but I would suggest you don't make
any noise until they're gone."

His breath laved her ear, pebbling the flesh along
her spine. She nodded her agreement and true to his

word, he released her. It took her a minute to breathe normally again, to stand steadily on her own as she heard the car start and the wheels spin away.

That's when, to thank the man who'd saved her life, she turned and triggered the microlight on her key-chain so that she could see her rescuer's face.

Sharp features…inky hair…bedroom eyes…

"Oh, no," Lucy moaned. "Not you!"

And then she passed out.

2

HE PULSED BEHIND HER as she clung to the iron bedstead on her knees, her bottom pressed into his groin.

He ran his hands over every inch of her body as if he were trying to memorize her, as if he might be tested as to the fullness of her hips or the firmness of her belly or the sensitivity of her breasts. Mmm, her breasts…he paid special attention to detail there, his clever fingers rolling and tugging the nipples into hard, sensitive points until she cried out in pleasure-pain. Keeping one hand busy tweaking them, he used the other to feather the auburn curls of her pubis with a light touch before dipping into her well.

"There," she murmured as he slid a single finger laden with her cream along her clit. "Oh, yes, sweet heaven…"

She'd never been so wet. Or so deliciously hot.

She glanced up across to the dresser with its antique mirror where she caught a reflection of their sexual dance. His bedroom eyes glittered at her via the mirror, and their gazes locked.

Slowly, he rocked into her…buried himself…pulled back so only his tip teased her.

No, no, fuck me deep and hard.

She mouthed the words she couldn't say. Had been raised not to say. She was too much of a lady. Though at the moment, she looked anything but. Wanton. A lust-filled, flushed-face wanton, her red hair wild and radiant. Her lust for him had transformed her into this creature of seduction.

She could tell he read her lips via the mirror, he could see his features when him and his gaze dropped so that he could see what his fingers were doing to her nipple. He squeezed hard and when she sighed, squeezed a little harder until she moaned.

Licking her lips, she rubbed her breast against his hand and lifted her tush and pushed back so they smacked together with an electric wallop.

He was doing what she wanted, doing her fast and hard. His slick cock plunged in and out of her. And his finger, oh, his finger was equally delicious, rubbing her with the same speed and intensity.

For a moment, she closed her eyes and became pure sensation. When she opened them, she caught him watching her again, his eyes narrowed into slits, his mouth open as he gasped harder and faster in perfect rhythm with his actions.

Letting go of the bedstead, she reached back with one hand through the vee of her thighs and let his cock slide her juices against her fingertips. Then she flexed her fingers and scraped her nails against his hard flesh, and the sensation seemed to undo him. He gave a low shout that unnerved her, and then plunged deep inside. .

Even as waves of pleasure rippled through her, she

stared straight ahead at their reflection, fascinated by his expression of pure lust....

Lucy blinked open her eyes to see the face she'd dreamed. Only rather than expressing lust, it reflected worry. *Over her.*

"You're awake."

She blinked and sniffed the air redolent with chicory coffee and andouille sausage. In response to the heavenly smells, her stomach growled.

"Where am I?" she asked.

"My family's fishing camp."

Fishing...water splashed somewhere nearby...and the room with nothing but a bed and some pegs on the wall seemed to shift just a little.

Confused, she murmured, "Feels like we're moving."

"We're on a houseboat tied to shore."

Lucy started to sit up until a sharp pain reminded her that she'd been shot. The breath whooshed out of her and she froze, her hands pressed to the mattress of the double bed.

"Let me help you."

Help meant he had to put his hands on her again. Hands about which she'd dreamed. Erotic hands. Hands that could do more interesting things than help her to sit up.

The thought made her blush.

"Well, at least you've got some color," he noted, which made her even warmer.

When he got her into a sitting position, she realized the wound was bandaged, and that she was still fully clothed. Despite the odds, she was alive and had him to thank for it.

"I don't even know your name."

"Justin Guidry. Don't worry about the wound. Flesh only." He helped her stand. "It'll smart for a while, but it'll heal nice."

"*Dr.* Guidry?"

He shook his head.

"You're an EMT?"

"Nope, not a paramedic, either," he said, heading for the doorway. "And you can call me Justin."

Now truly curious, Lucy followed him into a larger space that served both as kitchen and living room. There was a small couch and rocker set near the Franklin stove, plus a wooden table and a pair of mismatched chairs. The walls were of rough-hewn wood, relieved by a few framed photographs that looked like they'd been taken on family outings.

The wound twitched and she frowned down at the bandage. Conveniently, the thug had caught her flesh on her side between her crop top and flood pants. There wasn't even any blood on her clothing.

"If you're not a doctor or a medic, then how did you know what to do to take care of me?"

"Call it instinct, not to mention too much experience tending to my own and brothers' childhood injuries. Mama probably wished my brothers and I were dead many times over. Not that we used guns on each other. Well, maybe pretend ones."

His grin was self-effacing and contagious. Despite the circumstances, Lucy felt herself relax.

"Thank you, Justin."

"That would mean more to me with a proper introduction, so I would know who was thanking me."

"Lucy Ryan."

His grin widened. "Lucille. Fits you, *chère*. I always loved that name." As he took the coffee pot from the stove and filled a mug for her, he said, "Sit," and began humming the song "Lucille."

She didn't correct him. Didn't want to admit she wasn't a Lucille with all that exotic name conjured. She was just plain Lucy and had always been so. The Lucy guys were comfortable talking to. The Lucy who never caught a leer at the singles bars she sometimes visited with Dana.

Dana! Good Lord, by now her roommate must have discovered she wasn't home. That might not be of much concern, but when she didn't show up at the shop...

"You don't have a phone, do you?"

"Here? Afraid not."

"No cell phone?" Hers was still in her shoulder bag on the floor of her car.

"That would defeat the idea of having a few days of solitude, don't you think?"

Guilt flooded her. "Oh. I'll be out of your way as soon as I can find someone to get my car unstuck."

"I'm not complaining. But after we eat, we'll find a phone and a tow."

"Great. Thanks."

As she carefully cased herself into a chair at the table, her stomach growled again.

"Patience, *chère,* food's coming."

Lucy tipped back her mug and watched him take the iron skillet from the stove, links of andouille on one side, scrambled eggs on the other. He handled the food like he knew what he was doing. Unlike her. He split the breakfast on two plates, shoved one at her, then sat opposite her and began to eat. Lucy followed suit, not stopping until every morsel was gone.

"Delicious," she muttered after swallowing the last forkful.

"You really were hungry."

"All that stress."

"*That.* What was *that* about?"

"Just some guys stalking me."

"Oh, *chère,* you make a very bad liar."

She glared at him, and even though his expression wasn't accusing, said, "I didn't do anything wrong."

"I didn't think so."

"But I saw something I shouldn't have."

"And these guys wanted to keep you quiet."

She nodded and pushed the empty plate away. "And were willing to kill me to do so."

"Tell me."

She took a deep breath. Knowing she couldn't tell all of it, she said, "New Orleans, last night. It was in a courtyard." The vision was as clear in her mind as if she were seeing it now. "They were holding her arms…those two swine…and a third man knifed her to death."

"Did you know this third man?"

She shook her head. "I didn't even see his face. It was…like something out of a dream."

She wasn't going to tell him that by the time she arrived, the deed had been done and the woman's blood was spreading over her white dress as the accomplices let her fall facedown to the pavement. Or that she had seen the actual knifing in a dream that had awakened her an hour before. Lately, her dreams had been more frequent and more vivid than ever before.

Even so, she had arrived at the crime scene too late to save the victim…though not late enough for her own safety. As she'd stared at the body, she'd heard a shout, and the next thing she'd known the killer's accomplices were after her.

If she told him the whole truth and nothing but the truth, Justin wouldn't believe her. No one would.

Only her family would, and even they tried their best to make her stop tapping into the universal unconscious. Even her younger sister nagged at her to stop, though Lucy suspected that Jennifer was more intimately acquainted with the family curse of precognition than she would admit to. They all told her to ignore the dreams and they would go away. Only they never had. She'd really tried. Gran was the only one who really understood, because she'd had a lifetime of those dreams. Gran had suggested the day would come when she would want to develop her own gift.

So here she was, being taken care of by the man she'd made love to in her dream—make that dreams, plural—and she couldn't even warn him that she'd put him in danger.

Which made her feel awkward and intimidated.

"This courtyard," Justin said, "is it near your home? Would those two be able to find you easily if they went looking for you?"

"The murder took place near Canal, and I live right off Esplanade, so no, I don't think so."

"Opposite ends of the French Quarter," he mused. "So you chose to leave the city instead of going home. And you were on foot so late at night?"

"I walk for exercise," she hedged. She really did, even if that hadn't been her purpose last night.

"But your car was nearby."

Oops. Caught. Now what?

Not thrilled that he was questioning her like a cop with a prime suspect, Lucy took the offensive. "If you don't believe me, just say so!"

Justin stared at her for a moment before lowering his lids, stopping her from reading his expression. "I simply wanted the whole picture of what happened. More coffee?"

"Yes, please."

Lucy tried to relax again, but Justin Guidry was throwing her off-kilter in more ways than one. This unsettled feeling was due to more than a couple of erotic dreams featuring Justin that might link him to the dangerous situation she found herself in. He knew she wasn't telling him everything.

"Why run here to the bayou?" he continued. "Why not go straight to the New Orleans police?"

Irritation growing, she countered, "Why didn't you take me to a doctor and report a gunshot wound to the closest sheriff's office?"

"Impulse. It was only a flesh wound...and I wanted to hear your story before acting."

Pacified by his explanation, she echoed him. "Impulse, right. Me, too. I was too freaked out to think clearly. But afterward, I had time to give it some thought, and I *was* going back to New Orleans, straight to the police, when those creeps caught up to me. Now I don't know what to do." Another way of saying she was afraid, Lucy supposed. She didn't want to end up dead like that poor woman last night. "What about you? Are you going to turn me in?"

"Interesting turn of phrase," Justin mused. "But no. I don't want to bring you more trouble than you already have. I'm aware that things aren't always black or white, and secrets have a way of staying hidden in bayou country."

A thrill shot through Lucy, and she wondered if he meant something beyond her own situation.

She certainly wasn't a bayou country kind of girl, so the hiding part was only temporary. Sooner or later, she was going to have to return to New Orleans and deal with this mess.

But the ache in her side and fear made her opt for later.

LUCY RYAN was hiding something. That much was obvious. And she was afraid.

Looking out over the bayou where a lazy alligator

pretended to be a floating log, Justin let all his questions drift at the back of his mind.

Let her be, part of him thought. *But letting her be could get her killed, and I don't need another death on my conscience.*

Whether he liked it or not, he was going to have to go back to New Orleans sooner than he liked.

Hearing movement at the door, he turned to face Lucy, who'd insisted on cleaning up the breakfast dishes. Funny the way, each time he looked at her, she got more appealing. With her womanly hip pressed against the doorjamb, her gaze soft and her lips parted slightly, she was downright tempting.

He cleared his throat. "You ready to go to town?"

She met his gaze and lifted both hands. "These are the only clothes I have, so what you see is what you get."

Justin liked what he saw and wouldn't mind getting some of it for himself, he thought, his groin tightening.

Her soft body wasn't weak, merely inviting to a man's hardness. Her reddish brown hair made her complexion appear pale and delicate, despite the splash of freckles across her short nose. She had alluring gray eyes and a luscious bow-shaped mouth. The thing that tempted him most, however, was the smooth expanse of skin between her short top and low-cut pants. Skin that he'd had to look at and touch when he'd tended to the wound in her side. Skin that he longed to taste....

For a moment, he forgot about New Orleans and murders and guilt. For a moment, he wondered what it would be like to take her right there, in the doorway. For a moment, he felt so connected to this woman that he didn't even know what he might do to protect her.

And then the moment passed.

Fighting off the sexual haze, he decided any questions he had for her could wait.

"No bridge?" Lucy asked, looking around at the nearby bank in confusion.

"No bridge. No vehicles out here, either."

"Then how do we get to town?"

"Pirogue." He indicated the shallow, flat-bottomed boat tied to the houseboat.

"We're both going to fit in there?"

"Unless you want to walk through the swamp."

"Been there, done that," she muttered. "I have no desire to be a snack for an alligator."

He stepped down into the boat and held out his hand. She took it and then stepped in gracefully.

Still, the pirogue tilted slightly and her body brushed against his. He slipped his hands around her waist to steady her. Her eyes flared and he dared to think her reaction was personal. With one hand, he touched her cheek. A becoming color again filled her face. He rubbed the fleshy part of his thumb against her mouth until her lips parted, and she flashed her tongue over the full lower one as if in expectation....

What the hell was he thinking? They were standing in the pirogue in the middle of the swamp, breathing hard like two teenagers.

"You'd better sit down," he said more softly than he was feeling.

She nodded curtly, then dropped like a rock.

He untied the pirogue and pushed off.

"What's the name of the town?"

"LeBaux."

"You have people there?"

He immediately thought of his mother who would be ecstatic when he walked into the house with a woman on his arm. She'd been after him to marry for years. It wasn't that he didn't want to marry. He'd even felt love for a woman before, but that emotion had been fleeting. They hadn't meshed in the essential way two people needed to so they could make a life together. He'd drifted from one woman to another, and once he'd hit his thirtieth birthday still single, his mother had played matchmaker. He'd come to Sunday family dinner several times in the past year only to be treated to a prearranged companion. Nice women, but he'd felt no connection, not like he did with Lucy.

"My mother," he said, "twin younger brothers, two aunts and an uncle, assorted cousins." He'd been the only one in the family struck by the urge to move to the big city. "But to tell the truth, the whole town is like family. Anyone there would do anything for one of their own."

"I don't even know my neighbors," she admitted.

He shoved off, and as always, ever since he'd been a kid, nature held him in thrall.

They drifted through patches of duckbill grass and under cypress trees draped with Spanish moss. Here and there a water lily poked out of the water and wild flowers were scattered along the banks. Ahead, an otter swam, and overhead a blue heron wheeled and then dove to pluck a fish from the waters.

"This place is a paradise," Lucy said, turning to smile at him.

"A nice place to visit," he agreed.

"Under the right circumstances. I am a city girl at heart, though. I don't fit in here."

"Where do you fit?" he asked, thinking she'd fit perfectly in his bed.

"In a town house at the edge of the French Quarter. Dana Ebersole and I have been renting it for more than a year now."

He couldn't keep his disappointment at bay when he said, "Ah, so you live with someone."

"Oh, no, not like that. I mean, Dana isn't a man. She's been my best friend since we were kids. She's my business partner, as well."

A clarification that brought a smile to his lips. "What kind of business?"

"A shop in The Quarter called Bal Masque."

"Souvenirs."

"That, too. And masks for Mardi Gras. But mostly art pieces. We also give classes teaching people how to make their own masks."

"Are you an artist?"

"I went to art school. Not the same thing."

"So, some of those art pieces you sell—"

"Are mine," she admitted. "I lead the classes, as well. Dana was a business major. She's responsible for numbers and organization and advertising. In other words, she's the one who keeps us from going bankrupt.''

''The partnership sounds like a good match.''

''Very good. What about you?'' Lucy asked, glancing at him again. ''What do you do for a living?''

Not wanting to talk about his own work and the way he'd bungled his last case, he said, ''Look, we're just about there,'' hoping to distract her.

He saw her tense up and scan the bank ahead, as if she were afraid the thugs were waiting for her. But all that awaited them were the buildings across from the dock—a small grocery store and a diner.

''Don't worry, *chère,* I'll see that you're safe.''

Lucy glanced back at him. ''I'm not your responsibility,'' she said in all seriousness. ''As soon as we get my car, I'm off.''

He wanted to tell her that wasn't advisable, that she needed to give the flesh wound a couple of days to heal—anything to keep her with him a while longer, so he could see what she was all about, maybe even figure a way to help her—but he was fairly certain nothing he said would sway her. She seemed determined to be rid of him as quickly as she had the hoods who'd driven her into his arms.

He just had to decide if he was willing to let her.

3

When Justin turned from the languid stream of the bayou and poled up to a floating dock, Lucy anxiously looked around.

Part of her expected to encounter the men who'd chased her into the swamp waiting for her, guns drawn. But they were nowhere in sight. Lucy breathed a little easier.

Justin jumped out onto the floating dock first and with a few twists of rope against a wooden post tied up the boat. Then he hooked the hull to the dock with one foot and offered her a hand and a smile.

Heart fluttering at the way he was looking at her—like he knew, for heaven's sake, like he could read her mind about the dreams—Lucy reluctantly took his hand. Their physical connection was immediate and more intense than she would have imagined. Her palm felt scalded and as the sensation spread up her arm, she swayed slightly.

Justin easily pulled her right into him. The tips of her breasts brushed his chest, oh, so lightly, but her nipples immediately tightened and sent a warning to parts below. She squeezed her thighs together and awkwardly pushed past him.

"Are you all right, *chère?*"

The dock swayed under her, the motion adding to her already wonky stomach. "Yes, why?"

"You seem…well…a little breathless," he said, his voice low and warm as the sunshine. "I thought maybe the wound was letting you know it was there."

"Yes, the wound…" She was lying, of course. She'd forgotten all about being shot. She shrugged and forced a smile. "Just a twinge. It's fine now."

"Good." Placing a light hand at the small of her back, he started for the bank. "Watch your step here."

Her quick jump to dry land—make that *squishy* land—was inspired by the touch of his hand. Being close to Justin was difficult enough. Allowing him to continue touching her would drive her nuts because the intimate contact would remind her of the hot dreams.

And then all she would want to do is tear off his clothes and see if the sex was as good as she'd imagined.

Nothing could be that good, she argued with herself. At least nothing in her experience had led her to believe that sex could be in the fireworks category.

But wouldn't she like to find out?

No. *N-O.* She couldn't. Wouldn't. That would mean involving Justin Guidry in her life.

And that would mean involving Justin in the murder she'd witnessed.

Totally unacceptable. She'd got herself into this mess, so she was going to have to get herself out of it without involving anyone else with the murderers or the authorities.

First, though, she had to get her car out of the bayou.

"So where's the local garage?" she asked, as they walked along the edge of town. She was careful to leave a few inches of space between them. "I need to arrange for a tow truck."

"All in good time, *chère,* all in good time."

Now what was that supposed to mean?

Lucy thought Justin was headed straight through the center of town—all two blocks of double-story buildings, shops at street level, probably living quarters above. But he kept going, straight away from the bayou and toward a neat white house with a big front porch raised off the ground by cement-block stilts.

She looked around and noticed all of the houses were likewise equipped to deal with flooding from the bayou, the downside of living below sea level.

Suddenly Lucy felt Justin's hand at the small of her back again, and she practically raced him up the front steps to the door so he couldn't get a better grip on her.

"Hey, Mama, you got guests!" he called out, as he threw open the screen door.

The room was big and comfortable. Soft gold walls and dark rust couches were accented with brightly colored pillows and scarf valences at the long windows. A piano was set against one wall covered with dozens of framed photographs. Family, she thought, smiling.

A woman bearing an uncanny resemblance to Justin

flew through the doorway. Her hair was dark with a single silver streak tumbling down over her heavy-lidded brown eyes.

"Justin, my oldest, my most wonderful boy, is that—" she stopped dead in her tracks and gaped "—a young lady you have with you?"

Though she was obviously surprised, Justin's mother sounded pleased as punch, Lucy thought, amused at the way the woman addressed her son. There was great affection between the two of them, that was obvious from the big hug Justin gave his mother.

"Mama, I have brought home a woman in distress," he announced dramatically.

"Oh, my. How can I help?"

What in the world was he going to tell his mother? Surely he wouldn't alarm her with the truth.

As she stepped forward, hand held out, Lucy surreptitiously kicked Justin. "Lucy Ryan."

"Marie Guidry," the woman returned with a firm handshake. "What kind of help do you need?"

"All that rain…"

She gave Justin a glance to make sure he wasn't going to butt in with the part she didn't want told. His arms were crossed over his chest and his expression nonchalant. He was letting her tell it, thankfully.

"My car got stuck at the edge of the bayou and your son kindly brought me to town to get help. I need to have someone haul the car back onto the road and check it out to see that everything still works properly."

The last thing she needed was a breakdown on the way back to New Orleans.

"Oh, you poor dear. The rain was terrible…last night." Marie Guidry gave her son a look before adding, "That must have been a scare for you. Come in the kitchen and I'll get you something to eat. Food always makes a body feel better."

Lucy said, "I'm not hungry. Justin already fed me."

His mother's eyes rounded. "Oh, he did, did he?"

"What could I do, Mama, but feed a woman in distress?"

"So her car went into the bayou…at the fishing camp…how?"

"Well, not *right* at the fishing camp. Of course that's not possible." Justin suddenly sounded nervous. "Say, how about we have some coffee. Mama makes the best chicory coffee this side of New Orleans."

Justin was doing his best to distract his mother.

Though she turned back toward her kitchen, his mother asked, "And how would you know I make the *best* chicory? You taste every one in the parish?"

"Pretty darn near."

The warmth between mother and son made Lucy feel right at home. Maybe more at home than at her own parents' house. Not that her parents didn't care for her and her sister or welcome them home. They simply weren't as touchy-feely or as open with their emotions.

In the kitchen, a smaller, fairer version of Marie Guidry sat at the kitchen table and chopped vegetables, throwing them into a big pot. Justin introduced her to Lucy as Tante Jeannette.

"Nice to see that you have good taste in women, Justin. Your mother was beginning to worry that she was going to have to hire a matchmaker for you."

Startled by the woman's inference that she and Justin were an item, Lucy was just about to set her straight when she was interrupted by the heavy clump-clump of a male tread down the back stairs toward them.

"Ah, Stephen," Justin called out. "Just the man I was looking for."

"What, you need someone to cut up your bait for you?" asked the younger, taller, softer version of Justin.

"I need someone with a good strong truck and chain. I need to get a lady's car unstuck. The lady being Ms. Lucy Ryan here."

No smile crossed Stephen's lips as he gave Lucy the once-over, but he nodded in a friendly manner. "Should I round up Marcus, then?"

Justin lowered his voice to ask, "You know whose bed he's in?"

"I heard that," Marie Guidry said from across the room. She was at the stove pouring coffee in two mugs.

"Well, do *you* know?" Justin asked her.

"I try not to think about it." She gave Lucy an exasperated expression. "Three sons over thirty and not one of them married or even seeming concerned about settling down. I'll never have any grandbabies at this rate.''

"Don't worry, Mama," Justin said, "there's plenty of time for those."

"I mean before I'm too old to enjoy them."

"Watch what you wish for, Marie," Tante Jeanette warned her. "For all you know, Marcus already has a brood spread over the parish."

Justin sighed the dramatic sigh of a man who had an unwanted weight on his shoulders. "So, does anyone know where Marcus is or not?"

"Marcus is right here," rumbled a voice as its owner came through the back door.

His younger twin brothers were sort of identical in the way of stature and features. But while Stephen was neatly pressed and handsome in a quiet way, Marcus was unkempt and incredibly fetching with a day's growth and hair that hadn't yet been brushed.

Lucy could well believe he'd just gotten out of some lucky woman's bed....

Okay, so she had bed on the brain thanks to Marcus's captivating older brother.

Justin introduced Lucy to the twins and then sketched out her plight, leaving out the details just as she had done with his mother.

"We'll have your car out in no time," Stephen assured her. "You'll be on the way back to New Orleans before supper."

"If that's what the lady wants," Marcus said, arching an eyebrow.

Justin gave him a brotherly whack and said, "We're

on it, Lucille. Mama and Tante Jeanette, make sure the lady doesn't pine for my company in the meantime.'' He was about to follow the twins out the door, when he hesitated and looked back at Lucy, adding, ''Perhaps you ought to stay in the kitchen, *chère,* away from interested eyes.''

With that he left. Lucy felt the weight of curiosity aimed her way.

Thanks a bunch, Justin, she thought, facing the two women waiting for her to explain *that* mysterious comment.

''Is that my coffee?'' she asked, taking the mug from Marie. Quickly, she drank it down. ''Mmm, this *is* the best chicory. What's your secret?''

Lucy prayed Justin and his brothers would hurry, since she had no idea of how long she could keep his mother talking about her culinary prowess.

''THIS ISN'T GOING to be too hard,'' Stephen said, linking the chain under the back bumper of Lucy's car. ''Probably best if you get in and start it and put it in reverse. Then Marcus can pull easy-like while you give it a little gas.''

As if he hadn't gotten cars out of Louisiana bayou muck many times over the years, Justin thought.

But that was Stephen. Precise. Always going over the details ad nauseam. He didn't want to label his little brother obsessive-compulsive, but if the shoe fit... Even being an accountant reflected that part of his too-organized personality.

"Okay, we're set," he said, sliding behind the wheel and starting Lucy's car.

Stephen signaled Marcus, who put the truck in gear. And when Justin slid Lucy's transmission into in reverse, the car slid out of the sucky ground and back onto the gravel like a greased pig. When they both stopped, Stephen unhooked the chain and threw it in the back of the truck.

Marcus slid out of the truck, yelling, "Stephen, you drive. I'm going to catch a ride in the lady's car."

He settled into the passenger seat next to Justin, who waited until he'd backed up to the paved road and turned the car onto it before asking, "What's up, Marcus?"

"That's what I was wondering, B.B."

B.B. standing for Big Brother. Only Marcus referred to him in that casual way. Stephen…well, Stephen was Stephen.

"You're referring to?" Justin asked.

"Lucy Ryan. Lu-u-ci-i-ille."

Justin was annoyed by the way Marcus picked up on his nickname for Lucy. "Like I said, she's a lady in distress."

On the way over here to rescue her car, he'd drawn a graphic picture about what had happened the night before. The danger part, anyway.

His brothers had agreed to keep an eye out for the two men in case they came looking for Lucy. If they came too close and pushed too far, they would be sorry, Justin knew. No one messed with the Guidry boys in these parts and got away with it. They were a force to be reckoned with, Stephen included.

"So why do you think Lucille ended up out here?" Marcus probed.

"Here's where the pedal to the metal brought her. Simple as that."

"Maybe not so simple. Maybe it's fate."

"What? You think I should get involved?"

Marcus grinned at him. "Go for it, B.B."

"I meant as a private investigator."

"Well, not quite what I had in mind—"

"I know what you had in mind, Marcus. Playtime is always what you have in mind," Justin muttered, driving Lucy's car around to the back of the house where it would be less conspicuous.

Stephen pulled the truck up and parked it next to the car as additional camouflage.

Truth be told, he could use some playtime. And he hadn't missed a single one of Lucy Ryan's many charms. But while he had a lot of faults, taking advantage of a woman who was skating on thin ice wasn't one of them, so he might as well keep his libido in check.

"She's going to be flying back to her life in New Orleans as soon as I return her car keys," he said more to himself than to his brother.

"So don't give them to her yet…for her own good, of course. Or stop hiding at the fishing camp and fly home after her. Whatever it takes." Marcus slapped him on the back in a *go get her* manner.

Justin was thinking about doing that very thing as they headed for the back steps.

But was he really ready to face New Orleans?

To face his failure?

To face a ghost of his own making?

Laughter spilled out of the house, the inviting sound lightening his mood. Lucy's laughter. It sounded good. It sounded right.

It melted something inside him.

He hadn't had much to smile about lately outside of family, but Justin felt his chest tighten as he opened the kitchen door and went inside.

THE EDGINESS Lucy had felt on being left with the two women was completely gone by the time Justin and his brothers walked through the kitchen door. Marie and Tante Jeanette were delightful women who—though seeming to sense there was something wrong, that information was being kept from them—had done their best to put her at ease. After she'd made her call to Dana, assuring her that she was all right, Marie entertained her with stories of Justin's boyhood bayou exploits.

Laughter bubbled from Lucy as she listened to his mother relate how Justin at age ten had set out to feed the poor alligators because he thought that being so slow and all, they couldn't get their own food. So he'd taken a raw chicken into the pirogue and had wheeled it out to feed the alligators. That's when he'd learned how fast they could move when food was involved.

"So which story is Mama telling you?" Justin asked as he entered the kitchen.

"The one about the alligators," she said, trying not to snort.

He smiled, then gazed intently at her.

Suddenly breathless, Lucy said, "So you got my car out and it's okay, right?"

"Drove it with no problems," he said.

"So I should probably go."

Not that the idea thrilled her. It made her feel as if she were tied up in knots inside.

Going to the police with a slew of half truths wasn't her idea of something to look forward to. And if they tracked down the murderer and his accomplices and brought them in on charges, she would be expected to testify. Then she would have to lie and say she witnessed something she'd only seen in a dream, not in reality, because who would believe her otherwise?

How did she get around that?

Justin eyed his mama and aunt and then indicated Lucy should follow him to the living room.

Once there, he spoke in a lowered voice. "I think you should give it a day. Between the wound and those thugs looking for you—"

"I appreciate the offer, but I'm okay, really."

The longer she waited, the colder her feet would get about reporting the crime. And the closer she would come to psychic dreams she had no intention of fulfilling despite the fact that the man central to those dreams was so tempting.

"At least come back to the fishing camp so I can change the dressing."

"Why not just do it here?"

"I don't want to alarm Mama and Tante Jeanette."

"They already saw the bandage and asked me about it."

"What did you say?"

"I didn't tell them I'd been shot if that's what you're worried about. But I didn't exactly lie, either. I just said that it happened when my car went off the road and you patched me up."

"Quick thinking, *chère*."

Without warning, Justin palmed her bare flesh between the crop top and pants and cupped the area around the bandage with his hand.

Her body immediately responding, Lucy sucked in her breath. "What are you doing?"

"Feeling for heat that would indicate the wound is infected."

His touch was making her flesh curl with anticipation that had nothing to do with the wound. Her mouth went dry and her pulse raced.

She whispered, "I barely know the wound is there."

But touching her like that, Justin was making *her* hot, reminding her of the dreams. Every detail. She ought to step back, away from him, but somehow she couldn't. The heat spread randomly from where he still touched her to every other part of her body.

And he was feeling it, too. She could see it in his

expression that went from relaxed to taut in a matter of seconds. And in the way he was looking at her....

Justin's face seemed to draw closer and closer. Unless she was mistaken, he was thinking of kissing her. And then he seemed to think better, caught himself and pulled away.

Lucy felt her body sag with the relief of tension. She wrapped her arms around herself as if by doing so, she could protect herself against a renewal of sensation.

He was saying, "I don't think you ought to head back to New Orleans, just yet," when Stephen appeared in the doorway.

"Out front," he said.

Justin rushed to the front window, but held out a hand indicating Lucy should stay where she was. "Two strangers on foot casing the area. It might be them."

"The men who tried to kill me last night?"

He nodded. "What did they look like?"

"Stocky. Expensively dressed. One had thinning light hair, the other salt-and-pepper."

"That's them. Stephen, take Lucy upstairs and away from the windows."

As if someone had to tell her to stay out of sight! Lucy bit back a retort and told herself to be grateful that Justin was trying to help her. Obviously, his brothers, too. She guessed he'd gotten them up to speed when they went to fetch her car.

"What's going on?" Marie asked from the kitchen as Stephen guided her to the stairs.

"We're taking care of it, Mama," Stephen told her. "Just remember you don't know anything about any Lucy Ryan."

Marie's expression darkened and she murmured, "Oh, dear," as she shooed them up the stairs.

4

STEPHEN OPENED a door to a room that faced the street and said, "Justin's room, when he visits."

In spite of the danger lurking outside, Lucy felt a distinct tingle when she stepped into the room filled with memorabilia of Justin's youth. She shook the feeling away, and wondering what was going on outside, trying not to let her imagination get the best of her.

In a lowered voice so no one outside could hear, she said, "I thought the boat was simply the family fishing camp."

"It is. We all use it."

"So Justin lives...?"

"In New Orleans," Stephen said.

Which came as a knee-weakening surprise. The idea that Justin lived in the city—*her* city—where she could run into him at any time shot a thrill of anticipation through Lucy.

"What about you, Stephen?" she asked. "Do you live here? In this house, I mean."

He was standing in the doorway. Filling it actually. The Guidry boys were not small men.

"Across the hall," he said. "Well, most of the time.

I make a lot of trips to New Orleans for work. I hate hotels, so I keep a small apartment there, too."

"You never wanted to live in New Orleans full-time?"

"I never took to it, but that might be my fault for taking responsibility so seriously. It makes change difficult."

Lucy wondered what he meant by that. Did he mean taking care of his mother? Somehow she didn't think Marie needed anyone to take of her, and she certainly didn't seem to be the type to ask even if she did. Besides, Marie Guidry was probably only in her early fifties—the prime of life according to women's magazines.

It must be a Stephen thing, she decided.

"So does Marcus live here, too?"

Stephen laughed. "Nope. Too confining. In case you didn't guess, Marcus is the free-wheeling type. He has a shack down the road a piece, though he's here visiting often enough. At least a couple of times a week, actually. Nothing like home cooking, and Marcus takes advantage."

The small talk kept Lucy's nerves from stretching taut. What was going on downstairs? Though she heard muffled male voices, she couldn't make out what was being said.

She drifted closer to the window.

"Hey, stop," Stephen ordered.

She put a finger to her lips, pressed against the wall so that she wouldn't be seen through the glass. Then she managed to curl a finger under the sash and lift it slowly but surely until the voices drifted into the room.

"I told you, we haven't seen her."

"And if you had, you probably wouldn't say, right?"

Lucy recognized the voice as belonging to the guy who'd lost a shoe in the swamp.

"What is it you want with this…Lucy is it?" Marcus asked.

"That ain't none of your business."

Then Justin said, "You boys don't have any business here in LeBaux, so I suggest you take yourself back to New Orleans where you belong."

"We never said we were from New Orleans."

Lucy's stomach knotted at the mistake. Now they were going to know…

"You didn't have to say," Justin went on. "No one from bayou country wears shoes like those."

"They're Italian!"

"And useless. City shoes."

"He's criticizing my shoes!" the guy obsessed with his footwear complained.

"Forget the damn shoes!" his companion groused.

Justin mildly added, "I was merely making an observation."

Marcus didn't say anything to that. No one did.

Lucy drifted closer to the window and chanced a peek out. The four men below were squared off as if gearing up for a fight. Heart hammering, Lucy prayed there wouldn't be trouble. Dear Lord, she hadn't meant to bring trouble to anyone. These men were killers!

"Marcus, Justin!" came a female voice from below. "I thought you boys wanted some of my crawfish *étouffée*. Get in here now, before it gets cold!"

Marie! Lucy winced, then saw Marie's ploy worked. Marcus and Justin relaxed as if preparing to go inside, and the men backed off and headed for town.

Lucy paced, while Stephen merely waited patiently, quietly, so unlike his rowdier brothers.

A few minutes later, Justin opened the door to his old bedroom. "Go after them and see what they're up to," he told Stephen. "We'll stay here until they leave town."

"I'm on it."

The moment Stephen left the room, Lucy asked, "What if they decide to stay over?"

"Then you're stuck in this room with me for the duration."

"You like to give orders, don't you?"

"I like people to listen when I tell them to do something for their own good."

She got the feeling this was a criticism. *Of her?* "People listen," she muttered.

"Except when they can't stay away from a window."

"You couldn't have seen me."

"That's your opinion. If one of *them* saw you..." He shook his head.

"All right, stop trying to scare me."

Justin stepped close enough that his potent maleness seared her. "Are you scared, Lucy Ryan?"

"No," she lied, and sat herself in a creaky old chair near a makeshift desk and away from him.

Of course she was scared.

Scared, tired and sore.

The wound was making itself known once more and she wasn't feeling so good. As a matter of fact, her head felt a little woozy. Maybe she'd overdone it. Or maybe the adrenaline of the morning had simply worn off and exhaustion was finally overtaking her.

If she expected Justin to continue the discussion, she was disappointed. He remained at the window until a few minutes later Stephen's voice snaked up the stairs.

"All clear! You can come down now."

FLEETING SOUNDS of a mournful saxophone followed her as she sloshed through the rain. People were still coming in and out of restaurants. Even a torrent wouldn't stop those revelers—they would still hop from bar to bar, determined to make every moment count.

Angry and upset as she made her way home, she forced herself to hold together.... Crying could wait until she got to the privacy of her own bedroom.

A block from the town house, she heard a splash behind her, but when she turned to look, she saw nothing but a puddle in the sidewalk. Even so, her flesh crawled and she practically raced down the wet street.

Laughter echoed from one doorway...moans from another. She pressed her hands to her ears and ran.

*By the time she got to the courtyard, the rain had
intensified just like her pulse. Her heart was pumping
like she was in the midst of an aerobic workout.*

*Then she saw him waiting for her, rivulets of wet
sheening his face. For a moment, she faltered and
stared.*

*Then, when tears threatened again, she demanded,
"What are you doing here?" and pushed by him, keys
in hand.*

*But before he could answer, the quiet of the court-
yard was split by a sharp blast and she turned in time
to see him jerk and crumple to the wet flagstone....*

Lucy awoke with a gasp.

Blinking, she looked around into the shadowy corners and realized she was back on the houseboat.

The rains had started again. A waterfall was drumming against the roof. She concentrated on the
sound...closed her eyes for a moment...no, that was
a mistake, she realized as remnants of the dream tried
to claim her.

The psychic dream that was another warning like
the one that had come to her before the woman had
been killed!

Only this one had been about Justin being shot.

No...not again!

She steeled herself against giving into the emotion
of what she'd envisioned. Instead she focused on how
she'd ended up in Justin's bed again.

She remembered following Justin downstairs to face
his mother and aunt. They'd had to tell the women
everything, after all. Marie Guidry had listened with

an open mind, had wrapped her arms around Lucy in sympathy afterward, and declared her too warm. She'd demanded Justin take Lucy to a doctor for proper care.

Lucy had refused.

Justin had somehow gotten her to agree that she would come back to the houseboat with him to rest first before going back to New Orleans. He'd tended to her wound with an antibiotic salve and had threatened her with a visit to the emergency room if her fever spiked.

And then she had slept.

But though she was wet now—as if she'd really been rained on as in the dream—her body felt cooler than it had earlier. The fever seemed to have dissipated while she was sleeping.

"Feeling better?"

She gazed toward the doorway where Justin stood, his arms crossed over his chest as he watched her. Her heart began to thud with a distinct warning. Had he been standing there while she'd been trying to escape danger? While she'd seen him shot in front of her eyes?

"How long have you been there?" she demanded.

"Long enough to know you're awake, is all. You've slept half the day away."

Shaking away the remnants of the dream, she pushed herself up out of the bed and told herself it was up to her to change the future. "I need to get back to New Orleans."

"Not today."

With images of him shot in that courtyard haunting her, she said, "Yes, today."

"You need watching."

"I need to get into town as soon as possible!" she snapped. "So I can tell the authorities about the murder."

So she could get away from LeBaux before she put Justin's life in danger, before he could become another victim because of her.

"No, not yet."

She heard the steel in his voice and wondered at the contrast between this Justin and the one who cajoled smiles from her. His expression brooked no argument. There was something dark and determined and a little scary about him when he was like this.

"Y-you're keeping me prisoner?"

"I'm keeping you safe. Just until morning," Justin said. "You're in no shape to take care of yourself yet, *chère.* If you want to get out of here now, you'll have to swim to your car."

"A challenge?"

"No." He sighed. "I just hoped you could be reasonable is all."

Reasonable?

What was reasonable about being stranded with a man who invaded her dreams? Who threatened her peace of mind? Who was going to become even further embroiled in her mess and maybe die for it if she didn't do something to stop what was already set in motion?

But one look at Justin told her his mind was made up. And it wasn't like she could just leave on her own.

Surely she could resist him for another twelve hours. She'd never actually managed to change fate before—she certainly hadn't with the murder of that poor woman—still, how did she know she couldn't manage it?

Besides, the sun had already set and she wasn't about to go wandering around the bayou alone at night. Obviously Justin wasn't going to take her back to her car until he was good and ready. Until morning broke.

Twelve hours was a piece of cake, she told herself, even knowing it was a lie. Twelve minutes near him was enough to make her weak-kneed and all soft inside.

In the midst of her distress, she was distracted by a wonderful smell wafting into the room, making her stomach rumble. "What is that?"

"Mama's crawfish étouffée. Remember, she gave me enough for supper. You must be hungry."

"Starving," she admitted.

"Come and eat then."

He moved away from the door and she followed. Maybe food would give her the fuel to resist the man who occupied her dreams.

Maybe…

Once more she sat at his table, while he fetched the food. No matter that he hadn't cooked it himself, he seemed to wield pots and utensils like an expert, the same way he had that morning when he'd made her breakfast.

If she concentrated on the details, on the now, she didn't have to deal with the future yet. She didn't have to worry about psychic dreams that she maybe could or couldn't change.

"I'm not used to a man feeding me," she murmured as he filled her plate.

"What *are* you used to?"

"Having my dates take me to restaurants."

"You must eat in lots of restaurants."

"Only on occasion. Not *serious* eating, though," she assured him. "Just experimenting to see what's to my taste."

She'd never met a man she'd wanted to date more than a few times. And there hadn't been all that many of those, either. But she didn't mind. She liked having men as friends. Better than their trying to hook up with her when she didn't feel the vibe. She felt the vibe with Justin, all right.

A surreptitious look at him made her wonder what hooking up with him would be like.

Would reality have anything on her dreams? she wondered.

Or was Justin too good to be true?

She waited until they were both halfway through with their étouffée before she asked, "So what is it you do when you're not fishing?"

He arched his eyebrows and asked, "How do you know that's not the way I support myself?"

"Haven't seen any fish around here."

"Maybe I'm taking a few days off. It has been raining, in case you didn't notice."

"I noticed." She poked her fork into a piece of crawfish. "So, you're telling me you fish when you're in New Orleans, too? And don't try to deny you live there. Stephen told me you're just visiting LeBaux."

Justin's smile drifted off. "Stephen ought to keep his mouth shut about what doesn't concern him. At the moment, I haven't decided if I'm going back to New Orleans or not. My time there didn't prove to be all I had hoped for."

Frustrated that he wouldn't give her a straight answer, Lucy nevertheless decided to be satisfied with that. She didn't want to keep probing if it would hit another nerve as she'd so obviously done. She was never going to see Justin again once she left here, after all. The dreams were still in the realm of fantasy. They couldn't come true if she refused to have anything to do with Justin…the only way she could keep him safe.

Still, she was curious about just what Justin was doing out here alone in the bayou.

Hiding?

He certainly was complex.

He behaved as if taking care of a wounded woman was an everyday occurrence for him. He was gorgeous and entertaining, but beneath the charming facade, she sensed something different…something deeper and darker…something to which she responded to despite herself. Not that she liked being pushed around, even if it was for her own good. But that thread of steel in his veins when he wanted things his way had certainly surprised her.

Lucy remembered Justin saying something about the bayou hiding secrets. What secrets was the bayou hiding for him?

SOMETHING ABOUT Lucy Ryan got to Justin in a big way. No doubt it was the fact that she was a lady in distress and his natural proclivities were to help her. Especially now. He needed to feel right again.

But he wasn't ready to go back to New Orleans.

He watched her clean her plate like she'd been starving. A woman with appetites, he thought, wondering about other things she might hunger for.

"There's more on the stove."

"I would be eating with my eyes rather than with my stomach."

She had beautiful eyes. Large and gray and for the most part sincere so he could practically look right down to her soul. Rather he could, if he believed in souls. He wasn't sure what he believed in anymore. Certainly not in himself.

He rose and started to clear.

"No, I'll do it," she insisted, making contact with his hand as she reached for the same plate.

He thought she might pull her hand back—she'd been a bit jumpy—but she stood still, staring at him, eyes wide open. His pulse shuddered as he read desire in them. And fear.

She was afraid of him.

He let go of the dish.

"All right. It's all yours."

Sitting back at the table, he couldn't keep his eyes off her as she scraped plates into the garbage, then took them to the sink where a pan of soapy water awaited. He watched every movement of her hands—artist's hands, smooth with long fingers and neat dark red nails—and wondered what they would feel like washing *him*. His instant erection told him he would like to find out.

Not that he could. Or would. He was no good to her. No good to anyone, not even himself. The way his life was going, he could get them both killed.

The knowledge didn't stop him from fantasizing...from wanting to know every dip and curve of her body...from wanting to forget by losing himself inside her.

Justin shook himself. He was an idiot. He wasn't going to solve anything with sex. What he needed was a therapist and a couple of years on the couch. And a new profession, one that didn't get people killed.

"Done," she said, moving toward him and drying her hands with a dish towel. "You don't mind if I let the plates drain for a few minutes before drying them?"

"You're supposed to dry dishes?" he asked lightly, as if that were news to him.

Lucy came closer. "You yanking my chain?"

He'd like to yank her chain and anything else he could get hold of.

Instead he said, "This place is casual. The only reason I don't use paper plates is that it would give Mama a heart attack if she found 'em. She swears paper ruins good food.''

She cocked her head. "Do you always do what your mother expects of you?"

"Not always. A man has to have some say of his own. But I have to give her the plate issue, because I think she has a point.''

She reached over to wipe down the table and she was too close for Justin to ignore. He was filled with her woman's smell, her disturbing presence. And he was weak, after all. A mere man. He reached out and circled her wrist.

Leaning over the table, Lucy stopped what she was doing and met his gaze. Justin saw something in her features that reflected what he himself was feeling. Hunger for something more than food. The emotions were stronger than the fear he'd sensed earlier.

With the sound of rain tap-tap-tapping overhead, he pulled her to him. She didn't resist. A slight tug and she was cradled in his lap. They stared at each other for a moment more, a moment in which every fiber of his body stirred and responded to hers.

He wanted her, and unless he was out of his mind, she wanted him with equal craving.

"Oh, Lu-u-cille," he murmured before hooking a hand behind her neck and pulling her face to his.

5

THE FIRST TOUCH of Justin's mouth on hers was electric. Lucy gasped, the sound lost in the instant passion of the kiss. In those few seconds, all her good intentions melted away like sugar in the rain.

She kissed him back, savoring the taste of his mouth, the smoothness of his teeth, the strength of his tongue. His probing of her mouth reminded her of other probings, more intimate joinings. It reminded her of her dreams.

It was like a dream now—mouths melding, hands exploring. She quivered and her body responded with a rush of wet warmth when his fingers lightly explored the skin of her side—the good side, not the wounded one. He took her to a different place, away from trouble and fear. She became lost in the moment…in the heat…in the sense of euphoria of this being right.

But it wasn't right. She *was* wounded and he could be, too, because of her. That thought threaded its way through to her conscious. This was the first step toward making those dreams come true. The first step to hearing that shot ring out in the rain.

Lucy pushed at Justin's chest. He released her immediately and she bounded to her feet.

"That can't happen again!" she told him.

"If you say so."

"I just did!"

"Calm down, *chère*, I simply thought the attraction was mutual. I'm not trying to force you into anything."

"Like hell you're not. You're forcing me to stay here."

"Only for a few hours. I promise I'll get you to your car at first light."

Nerves jangled, Lucy decided at that moment that Justin couldn't force her to do anything. Let him think what he liked for now, but she was going to get off this houseboat and out of his life as soon as possible.

In the meantime, she looked for something to do and found a stack of magazines. "I hope you don't mind if I read. I'm wide-awake, and after that nap, it'll be hours before I can fall asleep again."

"The light won't bother me. I can fall asleep anywhere," he said, indicating the couch.

"Don't be silly. You have a perfectly good bed."

"You want to share?"

"I want you to use it." Grabbing a magazine, she plopped down on the couch. "When I get sleepy, I'll just stretch out here."

"If you insist."

Well, at least he was acting agreeable. Not that he went to bed right away.

But there were only so many things to do on a houseboat once the sun had set. And she had the couch and the reading light. Besides which, he'd been up since dawn without the benefit of a nap like she'd had.

Eventually Justin seemed jittery, as if having nothing left to do with himself was getting on his nerves. He looked tired, which he should be considering how early he'd risen that morning. She couldn't help noticing his eyelids were drooping more than usual.

"Are you sure about the bed?" he asked.

No teasing in his voice tonight. She could hear fatigue instead. Good.

"Positive," she said. "I'm probably going to be up for hours reading." And plotting, getting the nerve to do what she had to do. "The bed is all yours."

Still he hesitated, staring at her. She kept her expression neutral, gave him a little smile and hoped her "Good night" would do it.

"Night." He gave her a penetrating look before entering the bedroom and closing the door behind him.

And Lucy sagged with relief.

If he suspected anything, he wasn't acting on it. Just how long would it take him to fall asleep? Although she continued to flip through magazines, her eyes glazed over and she wasn't getting the content. She was too busy thinking about Justin.

Would he stay awake until she fell asleep? He could lie awake in bed listening for movement, for any indication that she wasn't simply reading. For how long, though? She only hoped she could stay awake for however long it took Justin to relax and go to sleep.

It was she who listened to the small noises Justin

made as he moved around the other room. And her imagination became engaged.

Closing her eyes, she could see him undressing, could imagine the long lean muscle of him as he removed garments one at a time. Though she'd never seen him naked in person, she'd seen all of him in dreams, and through them, she knew every inch of his too tempting flesh.

Sucking in a deep breath, she opened her eyes, but the images stayed with her, teasing her, keeping her from concentrating on the magazine in her lap, no matter how hard she tried.

The sound of the bed protesting as he climbed into it left her wanting what she experienced in her mind. The bed creaked with each toss and turn—and there were many of them—and she had to keep adjusting herself on the couch because she couldn't get comfortable, either.

Was he thinking of her just as she was of him?

Did he want her with the same intensity?

Did he want her at all?

He'd kissed her, yes, but that had been due to circumstance. Almost an accident.

He'd flirted with her all day, but flirtation seemed to be part of his natural charm, like he would do so with any woman on his radar.

Most likely he'd been working on automatic, not because he'd been turned on by her.

But he was certainly having a hard time settling down, she thought, hearing springs bounce yet again.

At this rate, he was never going to sleep, never going to give her the chance to escape.

Rain had started up again and was drumming against the roof. Great, another obstacle to getting home. Dana was probably going nuts worrying about why Lucy hadn't returned. Maybe she'd even alerted the police. All right, maybe not.

Lucy hadn't told her why she was in bayou country when she'd called from the Guidry place. Dana had jumped to the conclusion that she was there because of a man, and Lucy had let her roomie think what she would. She'd also assured her that she was okay and would be home before dark, but of course that hadn't happened.

And in her aggravation with Justin, she'd forgotten to call Dana with an update before heading back for the houseboat. When she got her car on the road, she would call from her cell phone, assuming her shoulder bag hadn't been stolen.

It was raining harder now.

As she listened, her heart seemed to beat in sync. She felt herself start to drift.

"Damn!" she whispered, forcing her eyes wide open.

She wasn't the one who was supposed to fall asleep....

Suddenly she realized the noises from the other room had stopped. No tossing, no turning, no creaking. She sat up straighter and listened harder, kept her ears tuned for the slightest sound beyond the rain. It was barely drizzling now.

Then she heard it…what was most likely a soft snore. At least she thought that's what it was. She listened harder. There it was again.

A snore!

Definitely a snore!

Heartened, she waited a few minutes to make certain Justin was sound asleep. Then she gently set down the magazine and got to her feet.

Each step she took was slow—a careful silent slide of a foot with a pause in between. By the time she got to the door, her pulse had quickened so that she could hear the blood rushing through her ears. What she was about to do was crazy and she knew it.

But what choice did she have if she didn't want to get Justin shot?

She wouldn't be a party to his getting hurt, maybe killed, not when she could possibly change things. With that thought, she determinedly opened the door just enough to squeeze through…and then she was alone with the night.

Getting through the bayou was the hard part, but she'd watched Justin handle the pirogue, so she at least had a clue what to do, which way to go.

Pausing for a second, she stared at the now-closed door, wishing that things could have been different, that she could have met Justin under more positive circumstances. That they could have treated each other like two people who were attracted to each other.

She'd like to know if he could truly create those fireworks for her.

Saddened that she would never know, Lucy moved

to the pirogue, then untied the rope fastening the shallow craft to the houseboat.

Oh, so carefully she climbed in and sat.

Pushing away from the houseboat, she gave it one last longing glance before turning her attention to the bayou and its secrets.

JUSTIN VIBRATED AWAKE.

"What the—"

There it was again, a gentle vibration under his pillow telling him someone was calling him. He checked his watch—close to midnight—and answered the phone that he'd taken with him from the house just in case Stephen or Marcus spotted the thugs looking for Lucy again.

He answered, "What's wrong?"

"Asleep on the job?"

Because it wasn't like Stephen to be flippant, Justin sat straight up. "They're back?"

"Wouldn't matter if they were. Your little bird has flown the coop."

"What?"

Justin bounded out of bed, and it was only after he threw open the door to find the main room empty that he remembered he was buck naked. Not that it mattered—there was no Lucy to startle.

"She's gone."

"I thought I said that."

There was engine noise in the background on Stephen's end. Justin asked, "You saw her?"

"Not in time to stop her. She was driving off. I heard the car and saw her from my room."

"You have to come get me so I can—"

"Already done. I'm on my way. See you in a few minutes."

The engine roared louder just before the cell phone went dead.

"Great. Just great."

Justin wasted no time in getting dressed. Stephen would be as good as his word. Even so, even though Lucy only had a short head start, she would be far ahead of him.

What would she do when he caught up to her? Tell him she didn't need his help? Probably. Apparently she didn't want his help.

So why was he bothering?

Unfortunately, he wasn't raised to ignore a lady in distress—or anyone in distress, for that matter.

Hearing an approaching motor, he stepped outside and waved his brother down. Stephen had barely pulled up to the houseboat before Justin jumped inside. And off they went, though not headed toward home.

"Marcus is pulling your car around to meet us."

"That'll save some time."

"So you're going to go after her. I thought you weren't ready to go back to New Orleans."

"I'm not."

"Then why go? Okay, dumb question. Your chance for a do-over."

"Right." As if anything could make up for a lost life. "A do-over."

Not to mention that he didn't mean to let Lucy Ryan get away from him so easily.

"C'MON, C'MON," Lucy muttered into the phone.

Having stopped for gas and some much-needed caffeine—the stress must have gotten to her, because her body begged to be shut down—she was anxious to get back on the road again. The only audible response she got when the phone at the other end stopped ringing was Dana's voice mail.

"Hi, we're not available to come to the phone at the moment, but we don't want to miss your call," Dana said in that breezy way of hers. *"So when you hear the beep, leave your name, number and a brief message. Ta."*

Leaving Dana a message wasn't exactly what Lucy'd had in mind, but it would have to do.

"Hey, Dana, I'm on my way." Lucy tried to keep her voice equally breezy, as if she were having a great "time-out" from her real life. "I'll probably beat you home. At least I hope you're having a good enough time to be out half the night. See you whenever."

Lucy hung up the phone, took another sip of her coffee and hurried back to the car.

She would have called Dana from her cell, but not only was it missing, so was her shoulder bag.

Luckily she'd had her wallet—and therefore her identification—in her pocket. No doubt the men who'd come after her had taken the bag from the car the night before. She would have loved to see the frustration on their faces when they came up empty.

So where was Dana at this hour? New boyfriend?

Lucy was actually glad her roomie wasn't home. She was a mess and on seeing that, her best friend would demand answers she wasn't prepared to give. She didn't want to involve anyone else in her troubles. Besides Dana would feel obligated to tell Jennifer and her sister would be obliged to tell her parents.

No, better that she tell Dana everything once the bad guys were where they belonged.

So she would go home and shower and wash her hair and put on some clean clothes so she would look presentable before facing the police. Even so, she was worried whether or not they would believe her, especially since she hadn't gone straight to the nearest police station.

She would cross that hurdle when she got to it. She would keep a positive attitude.

Entering New Orleans, she headed straight for the garage where she parked her car. The streets in the French Quarter were too narrow and busy to provide parking where one lived. Walking the block and a half home, she was uncomfortable. Jumpy. And even though it was no longer raining, she was still reminded of that last dream.

Glancing back over her shoulder at the empty street, Lucy lengthened her stride, telling herself she needed to quell her imagination. She entered her courtyard and started across the flagstone.

"What took you so long, Lucille?" came a voice from the shadows.

Her heart skipped a beat as a determined-looking Justin Guidry came right at her.

6

THOUGH JUSTIN was relieved to see Lucy in one piece, he wasn't going to show it and let her have the upper hand.

Her stiff "What are you doing here?" didn't sound at all appreciative of his concern.

"The question is…what are you? I'm sure I remember your promising to wait until morning."

"I thought better of it. I couldn't sleep."

"So you stole away in the night like a thief?"

"I'm no thief!" she insisted, turning on her heel and heading across the courtyard. "I just borrowed your boat and left it at the dock in town."

Following close behind, he said, "So you stole away in the night like a borrower?" He shook his head at the play on words. "Nope, that doesn't work for me."

Lucy glanced back at him. "Sorry if I inconvenienced you. But I don't understand why you're here."

"In some cultures, if you save a person's life, you're responsible for it."

"This isn't some cultures," Lucy informed him, stopping in front of a door and sorting through the keys in her hand. "So let me be responsible for myself. I'm okay with that."

"Maybe I'm not."

"I don't get it."

"Apparently you don't." Justin stepped closer, wanting to yell at her rather than remain calm and reasonable, but yelling would get him nowhere. "You're dealing with a dangerous situation, with dangerous men. You can't handle that yourself."

"So I'll let the police handle it." She unlocked the door and opened it, but didn't immediately go inside. "After I clean up, I'm planning on going to the police and telling them everything I know."

"Which is not necessarily the best idea."

"Why not? What do you have against the police? You haven't wanted me to go to them from the first."

"The police can't protect you in a situation like this."

"And *you* can? But why would you want to? And don't give me the responsible for my life ploy—"

"I'm a private investigator," he finally admitted. "This is what I do."

"You're a P.I.? Why didn't you say anything?"

Not wanting to go into it, Justin said, "I was trying to have a time-out."

Lucy gave him an intense look as if she was trying to get inside his head. "Why do I think there's more to this story?" she asked.

"Maybe I'll tell you about it sometime." Now certainly wasn't the right time to tell her he'd let a client get killed—which would be a real confidence builder.

How could it not be when he'd lost confidence in himself? "Right now, let's concentrate on *your* situation."

She thought about it for a moment. He could practically see the wheels turning in her head as she tried to make up her mind. There was something in her expression…something that stirred him. And suddenly her answer became even more important to him than he'd realized. Not that he could explain it, not even to himself.

"Come inside," Lucy finally said, taking the lead.

Her capitulation let him breathe normally again when he hadn't even realized he was holding his breath. With a sense of relief, Justin followed her inside, entering something of a fantasyland.

While the furniture was mostly plain and upholstered in a pale butter-yellow, the walls were a deep, brilliant blue and decorated with a few colorful Mardi Gras posters and masks—sequined and feathered and papier-mâchéd. The effect was stunning, the room a reflection of the talented woman who'd decorated it.

"Can I get you a drink?" she asked.

"A soda would be good."

She disappeared into the kitchen and came back a moment later with two cans. "Your choice."

He picked the orange and she opened the top on the root beer. She tilted back her head to take a drink, and for a moment he was mesmerized by the lovely length of her neck.

A neck he would like to nuzzle and taste….

To dispel the thoughts wandering in the wrong direction, Justin opened his can and took a long slug, as if that would cool him down.

Lucy said, "You know, while I saw the murder, I have no clue as to the identities of the men involved. Or of the victim, for that matter. So if I don't go to the police, where do you propose we start?"

"With the victim. Murder victims get media coverage."

"So if we figure out the identity of the woman who was murdered, then what?"

"Then we investigate *her.*"

She thought about it for a moment before saying, "You think you can do it—find the murderer, I mean?"

"Like I said, that's what I do."

"Then what?"

"Then we turn him over to the police. I have a couple of contacts in the department."

"I thought cops and P.I.s didn't get along."

"Not in the movies. Without conflict, you wouldn't have a story. This is real life…though every case is different when you're talking cooperation. How much credibility a P.I. has depends on his reputation."

"All right, I'll try it your way first."

"We can start in the morning."

"Where do I find you?"

Justin moved in on her, saying, "Actually, that won't be hard since I'm taking you home with me."

Her eyes widened and he swore he saw a touch of panic in their depths when she said, "I don't think so."

"Hard to protect you long-distance. So if you insist on staying here, I suppose I can bunk on the couch tonight."

"Why would I need protection *here?* Those two don't know where to find me."

"Don't be too sure of that."

"I had my wallet and therefore all my identification in my pocket."

"But they could have gotten a look at your license plates," Justin told her. "You don't know what kind of contacts these men have. They could already have this address."

Lucy's eyes widened in alarm. "Oh, no. Then Dana is in danger, too."

"Does she look like you?"

"No."

"Then I don't think it's a problem. They got a good look at you, remember, and they're not going to involve yet another person if they don't have to. Though if you want to be extra-safe, you could suggest Dana stay with relatives or a friend for a few days."

Justin could see that he'd upset Lucy. Now she was worried for her friend and for herself. He wanted to take her in his arms and tell her everything would be all right, but he didn't trust himself to make the comforting gesture without letting it turn into something else. Besides, he could only do his best. Nothing in life seemed guaranteed lately.

Though Lucy hadn't given him an answer about staying at his place, Justin decided to take that for granted. "You said you wanted to get cleaned up."

"Right. I'll be quick. Give me twenty minutes and I'll be ready to go."

Lucy hurried up the stairs and Justin fought the temptation to follow her to see that she was safe. He had to give her some credit. If he tried to be too protective, he would suffocate her, and Lucy didn't seem to be the type of woman who would tolerate smothering.

Instead, he wandered around the room and inspected her collection of Mardi Gras masks, assuming they were all collectables. But when he got close enough to one of the masks, he found a tiny L.R. executed into the edge of the design and realized Lucy herself had created it. He kept going and found her initials on other masks.

Add talent to her other attractions and Justin was sorry they'd met under such terrible circumstances.

He was pondering life's little cruelties when he heard Lucy coming down the stairs. She wore low-rise white jeans that molded her lower body like a second skin. Her red halter top was equally snug and revealing. He could see the lower part of a fresh bandage on her wound. Too bad she was carrying a shirt that he was certain she would soon put on to hide the sexiness of the outfit. To his relief, she was also carrying an overnight bag.

"You clean up nice, *chère,*" he said.

"Hair's still damp," she said, dropping the bag to put on the shirt. "But if it's still raining, I figured I would be drying it for nothing."

Before they could get on their way, the door opened

and a sleek blonde walked in. Her pale beige silk pant-suit, damp from the rain, clung to her womanly curves. Her long hair was scraped back from an angular face and fastened in a twist. No doubt this was Dana.

"Hey." The skin around her blue eyes crinkling with what looked like worry, Dana looked from him to Lucy. "You're home. For the moment anyway."

Clearly Dana had caught sight of the overnight bag.

"Yeah, I was, uh, going to Justin's place," Lucy said in a rush as she picked up her bag. "Um, this is Justin Guidry. Dana Ebersole."

"Nice to meet you, Dana."

Dana's eyebrows arched and her full lips curved into a broad smile. "You, too."

"We were just about to leave, but—"

"No buts. You go, girl."

Obviously uncomfortable, Lucy ducked her head and said, "I'm not sure when I'll be home. Can you take care of the shop again tomorrow?"

"Sure."

"I'll make it up to you, I promise. And one more thing."

"What?"

"Go stay with your sister for a couple of days. I mean starting tonight."

Dana gaped, then said, "Okay, now you have me worried. What's going on?"

Justin said, "Just a precaution—" when Lucy kicked him and interrupted.

"Trust me when I tell you it's better if you don't

know anything. Just get out of here for a few days. I'll call you when it's okay to come back.''

"What are you into, Justin?" Dana asked, her expression suddenly darkening with suspicion. "What have you gotten Lucy into?"

Before he could answer, Lucy said, "Not Justin, me. I've gotten *him* into something."

"You?"

"Yeah, um, something I saw."

"What? You mean you're doing a disappearing act—and want me to do the same—because of one of your visions?"

"Visions?" Justin echoed, suddenly alarmed.

Lucy ignored him. "Dana, please. Just trust me on this."

"All right. I'll bunk with Laura. She'll be thrilled when I show up on her doorstep at this hour, but I'll do it if it'll make you feel better."

"It will."

"And if you promise to give me a detailed explanation later."

"*I will!*"

"All right then."

Justin listened to the exchange with his jaw clenched.

A vision? What the hell was that supposed to mean? He wasn't liking this new turn of events.

But he waited until they were back on the street and headed for his car to ask. "Okay, *chère,* what's this about a vision?"

"It wasn't exactly a vision."

"Then what actually was it?"

"A dream."

Lucy walked ahead of him, as if that were the end of it, but Justin wasn't letting her off that easy. None of this was computing. Two strides and he caught up to her.

"What kind of dream?" When she didn't answer, he said, "I think an explanation is in order."

"All right. I have psychic dreams."

He grasped her upper arm and stopped her right there, demanding, "What about the murder?"

"I saw it in a dream."

His curse made her wince.

"I don't believe this," he growled. "Then why were those two after you?"

"Because I tried to stop the murder from happening. I was too late. The woman was already on the ground...." Lucy's face was distraught. "But I guess they thought I saw it all. The man who stabbed her sent them after me."

"You mean the one who stabbed her *in your dream.*"

"He was standing over her and holding the knife in person, too. I think that qualifies."

"But you were planning on going to the police based on what you saw while you were dreaming."

"If you're the one who had the dream, what would you do?"

Justin thought about it for a moment. Psychic dreams? He wasn't sure he believed in them. But who was he to say it was impossible? Lucy obviously believed in them. Whatever brought her to that spot near Canal Street got her a bullet wound and two thugs looking to finish her off for her trouble.

"I would have to get to the bottom of it," he admitted. Not wanting to discuss it further on the street, he said, "Let's get going."

The car was just ahead. He popped the trunk and tossed her bag in. A moment later, they pulled away from the curb.

Lucy Ryan was in real danger, Justin knew, and keeping her safe was all that mattered.

JUSTIN LIVED and worked on the other side of Canal in the Warehouse District, far enough from her place to make Lucy relax a little. They would never look for her here.

Justin called a loft in a converted warehouse home. The walls of the main room that weren't brick were painted a burnt orange. His sofa and chairs in brown leather looked old but big and comfortable, and surrounded a well worn Oriental rug. The tables were heavy—real wood—as were the cabinets in the open kitchen area. The whole place had a comfortable, lived-in feel, one Lucy appreciated.

She wandered over to the window and looked out on the city she loved. Part of her wanted to flee and never come back. But she knew that wouldn't solve anything. Her dreams would simply follow no matter where she went.

"You look like you're going to have trouble sleeping,'' Justin said. ''A drink might relax you. What's your pleasure?''

She almost said *you,* but caught herself before letting the incriminating word loose. The last thing she wanted was to look like a fool.

''Tea, if you have some,'' she said, instead.

''I'll put on the kettle. You pick the tea.''

Justin set a box on the counter, and Lucy went to investigate. It was old and made of heavy wood like the furniture. The inside was lined with velvet and filled with a half-dozen types of tea. She chose a raspberry herbal tea that she thought would help relax her.

Then she watched Justin move around his kitchen area. He looked as comfortable here as he did on the houseboat. And as sexy. He'd kicked off his shoes and was in stockinged feet, his shirttails were hanging free of soft old jeans that molded to his bottom and thighs, and he'd undone several buttons of his shirt, revealing enough skin to make a girl fantasize even if she hadn't already been having dreams about him.

Then he turned and caught her staring, and for a moment the breath caught in her throat.

Could he possibly know what she was thinking?

But when he spoke, it was simply to say, ''Here's your hot water.''

Blinking, she stared at the mug he was offering her. With a start, she took it and immersed her tea bag. ''You're not joining me?''

''Tonight I need something stronger than tea.''

He crossed to a cart in the main room stocked with bottles and glasses. He poured himself a whiskey and threw back the shot in one swallow, then refilled the glass before capping the bottle and returning into the kitchen area.

Great. Now she was driving men to drink.

She took a tentative sip of her tea and felt it soothe its way down to her stomach.

Then his "So tell me about the dreams" made her stomach clench.

That's why he'd needed the whiskey, she was sure—because he was thrown by the mere mention of the damn dreams.

"I've had them since I was a child," Lucy told him. "But from the first, my parents discouraged me from sharing them or even believing in them. They told me to forget about them…as if I could."

"You tried?"

"Are you kidding? Every kid wants to be normal. Even my little sister Jennifer bugged me to repress them because people would think I was a freak. Only Gran understands what it's like to be different. She's got a heck of a lot more psychic ability than I do."

"So you're the only one who inherited this…gift?"

"You mean curse? The only one who will admit it, anyway, though I've often suspected Jennifer knows what's going to happen before something actually does."

Now he was going to laugh at her…make fun of her…think she was a freak.

But he didn't as he leaned against the counter opposite her. They were a full three feet apart, yet she felt his presence as powerfully as if he were touching her. His expression serious, he studied her closely for a moment before downing the second shot of whiskey.

Yep, just thinking about her having psychic dreams was driving him to drink....

"Have you ever tried to do something with this ability of yours?" Justin asked.

"Like what?"

"A lot of psychics help the authorities to find lost children...solve murders."

"I don't have that kind of ability to control what I see. The dreams just come. I never know when or what I'll see."

"I'm assuming this is your first murder?"

"Thankfully. And I hope my last."

"What else do you dream about?"

"Usually things that bring about an emotional response."

"Like?"

Like making love with him. Lucy flushed. Wouldn't he be astounded if she told him she'd dreamed of him before meeting him? Even more astounded if she described the dream. Of course she couldn't ever tell him that.

"One time, I dreamed my dad was going to have a car accident and I convinced him to take a different route home."

"So he avoided the accident."

Lucy shook her head. "He wasn't hurt badly, but he just couldn't avoid his fate."

A fact that terrified her. She couldn't let Justin get hurt, or worse, one of the reasons she'd agreed to work with him. Maybe if they could identify the murderer…a long shot, but what choice did she have?

"You look like you're ready to go to bed," Justin said.

"I am exhausted."

"The bed is upstairs."

"You're not giving me your bed again."

"Sure I am. Don't worry about me. I've slept on that couch many a night. And I'm not about to fall asleep anytime soon."

Remembering she'd used the same ploy earlier, Lucy asked, "You're not going to try to escape, are you?"

"Where would I go?"

"Anyplace to get away from me."

"Would I do that, *chère?*"

"Other people have."

"Other men?"

"Other men," she agreed.

"I'm not just any man."

He certainly wasn't. She'd known that from the first dream. And no other man had taken her curse in quite the same stride. A couple of whiskeys was nothing compared to the way the other men she'd told had reacted—as in running as fast and far from her as they could.

"All right, no argument," she agreed. "I'll take the bed tonight."

"Good."

But as she stooped to pick up her bag, their hands met on the handle. Lucy froze, but her insides were dancing. No, no, nothing to get excited about. Ignoring the charge to felt, she straightened, letting Justin take the bag for her.

Only when he turned his back to head for the stairs did she gasp for breath.

"Something wrong?" he asked.

"Nope," she gritted out. "Coming."

She followed Justin to the metal spiral staircase, keeping a couple of yards distance between them. Not liking the subtle sway of the freestanding stairs, she took them gingerly, refused to look down and was relieved when she got to the top.

"Bathroom is around the corner," he told her. "Make yourself at home."

Like she could relax with Justin nearby.

Only when he descended the staircase, did she start to breathe normally. Would it always be like this? she wondered. Her jumpy as long he was around?

She opened her bag and removed her pajamas—red silk crop pants and a crop top, both with lace trim—the most conservative thing she had for sleep. Assuming she would get any.

A glance at the metal-framed bed made her knees go weak.

The bed in the dream...her facing the footboard, Justin behind her doing wonderfully erotic things....

Turning off the bedside lamp so she couldn't see the bed, Lucy undressed in the dark, her imagination engaged. She could almost feel Justin in here, kissing her, making love to her.

Her nipples tightened and warmth spread from her

center. She tried fighting the inviting sensations, but when she looked over the railing, she saw Justin stripping off his shirt. She moved closer—just close enough to see him through the iron rails without his being able to see her—and watched.

He'd already thrown a pillow and sheet on the couch. Despite his protests to the contrary, he was getting ready to go to sleep. His jeans came next. Other than a pair of skimpy briefs, he was the next best thing to naked.

Warmth pooled between her thighs and she slipped a hand down the front of her silky bottoms until she touched the damp material there. A thrill shot through her, from her fingers to her center.

Below her, Justin shut off the light but the windows weren't covered and the moon cast a blue glow into the room, so she could still see him from her protected spot in the dark. He threw himself onto the couch, one hand over his head, the other moving down his stomach to disappear inside his briefs.

Her eyes widened as his hand moved and his body responded.

Good Lord, he was masturbating!

She couldn't help her own hand from following suit. Fingers slipping along her skin under the silk, they pushed easily through the thick wetness at her entrance. One touch to her clit and she bit back a cry of pleasure. She stroked deeper inside and pressure immediately began to build.

Below, Justin was silently stroking himself. Pieces

of her dreams floated in her own head—she imagined her and Justin together, pleasuring each other.

Her flesh swelled and she moved her fingers faster, over her clit and through her folds...back and forth... holding her breath so she wouldn't cry out...wanting more than anything to have Justin inside her just like in her dream.

Below, he was tensing on the couch, and she knew he was about to come.

In her mind, she felt him again, entering her from behind.

Below, she saw him dig his heels into the couch and arch, his body tensing.

Another stroke of her clit and she was there with him...coming...coming...spent....

She must have made a sound, because Justin rose to an elbow, his face angled upward.

Her heart was pounding so loudly that surely he must hear its frenzied beat.

Surely Justin saw nothing. He turned on his side, punching the pillow as if in frustration before finally settling down.

Still, she didn't dare move until she was certain he was asleep.

The soft snore gave him away once more.

As carefully as she had when she'd made her escape earlier, Lucy backed up toward the bed, sliding one foot behind the other. The mattress hit her legs and she sat, finally giving in to the dizzying sensations.

What had come over her? She'd never done anything like that before. She'd be horrified if Justin knew. She'd invaded a private moment.

So why didn't she feel bad?

Actually, she felt good. Wonderful, even. The sexual tension that had been mounting since she'd met him finally was released.

Now maybe she could get on with things. Put her mind where it belonged—on the murderer and how to find him.

With that satisfying thought, she stretched out on the bed, and listening to the rain pelting the windows, drifted off into a deep sleep.

7
___

AS THOUGH THE RAIN washed away her natural inhibitions, she lifted her skirt in invitation. He watched with a heated gaze as the material climbed and clung wetly to her curves and tangled around her legs.

Despite the weather forecast—tropical storm watch—she'd run into the rain and the garden and he'd followed.

It was a game. Truth or dare.

She hadn't wanted to tell the truth, so she'd taken him up on his dare.

She wasn't wearing panty hose…or panties, either…just the skirt and a camisole-type blouse that might as well not be there for all it protected her when wet. Glancing down at herself, through the fine material, she could see the dark aureoles of her nipples almost as if she were wearing nothing at all. Her nipples peaked and pushed at the transparency while her fingers tugged and pulled at her skirts until she was exposed to him.

With a groan, he unzipped and revealed himself…long and hard…veins prominent…an impatient purplish red.

He was as ready as he was going to be, so she

leaned back against a tree, unfolded her legs and, as she inhaled the scent of magnolia, he moved over her and pushed himself inside.

With her spread wantonly for him, his cock slid easily to the hilt. When he had her pinned, she curled her legs around his thighs, holding him fast.

He slid slowly out so that just his soft tip was buried in her folds. She made a small sound of complaint and he laughed before slowly sliding back in, filling her fully once more.

Better, she thought with a sigh.

She stretched out for him, her hands tangled around tree limbs on either side of her for balance. She arched her back hard, shoving her breasts toward him. He showed his appreciation, cupping them, rubbing his thumbs over her nipples, setting her on fire inside.

She wanted to come right then.

He wouldn't let her.

Every time her breathing quickened for more than a few seconds, he stopped moving his hands, stopped moving his hips.

How could he be so cruel?

She would see to the matter herself then....

Letting go of the tree, she arched back even farther, her long hair dripping with water behind her. She cupped her own breasts, tugged at her own nipples, and was gratified when his breathing matched her own.

He liked watching, she thought with a smile.

No longer slowing down, he made his forays into

her shorter and sharper. His hands found her buttocks and steadied her as he drove himself faster and faster.

She lifted slightly so she could watch his face…his bedroom eyes…and when they began to cloud over, she flashed her hand between them to find her clit. She was ready to come, and at the first stroke, she felt the strong, deep pulls that signaled release.

"Yes," she murmured. "Now. Now!"

He came with a shout and she pitched over the edge with him, feeling as if she were sliding down a rushing waterfall.…

Awakening with a start, Lucy realized she'd been dreaming again. Another psychic erotic dream in which Justin was the star.

What in the world was wrong with her?

Why couldn't she stop having these visions…or wanting more than anything to make them come true? If she were a man, she would be walking around with a perpetual hard-on. She hadn't known a woman could be this horny.

Slipping out of bed, she moved to the railing and glanced over it, wondering if she would get a glimpse of a nearly naked Justin in broad daylight.

No luck—he wasn't there.

A cold shower helped her regain some of her sanity. Afterward, she bandaged her wound, which was healing nicely—not so much as a twinge when she touched it.

Then she quickly dressed and twisted up her hair, securing the masses in place with a fancy hair clip.

Feeling better prepared to face the man haunting her sleep, she went down to find him.

The smell of freshly brewed coffee drew her to the counter where a mug sat in front of the coffeemaker as if awaiting her. She was filling it when she heard the door and turned to see Justin enter, carrying a white bag.

"I hope you like beignets for breakfast."

"My mouth is already watering."

But her mouth was watering for him as well as for the freshly fried puffs of pastry doused with powdered sugar. He looked equally yummy in a pale gold shirt and tan pants, sunglasses tucked up in his dark hair.

"I'm glad you approve," he said with a slow smile. "I've been gone long enough that I don't have anything safe to eat in the fridge. I thought we could get started on these, do a little research, and when we couldn't stand it any longer, we could go out for a proper meal."

"Whatever you say," Lucy told him, meaning it.

If he wanted to eat *her,* or vice-versa, she would be hardpressed to deny him.

But she settled for the beignets and coffee, laughing as they both covered themselves with powdered sugar. The breakfast sweets were impossible to eat without making a mess.

Lucy was careful not to get too close to Justin as they cleaned up the counter and poured fresh mugs of coffee, but then her plan to keep her distance went astray when they settled in front of Justin's computer and their knees knocked together. Swallowing hard, she scooted her chair a few inches away from him to give herself room.

Though one dark eyebrow raised at her action, Justin didn't comment on it. Instead, he said, "I figure we should check yesterday's *Times-Picayune* online first, see if there's a report of any body being found."

The seriousness of their quest drove away frivolous thoughts, and Lucy asked, "What if there isn't, Justin? Will you think I'm crazy?"

"I already think you're crazy, *chère*…in the nicest of ways."

She relaxed a little. "No, really."

"If we can't find it here, we'll use other avenues. I have sources."

But other avenues didn't prove necessary. Skipping past the latest election headlines with councilman-at-large Charles Cahill decrying Louisiana senator Carlin Montgomery for being a suspect in a bribery case, Justin easily found a headline that read "Murder In The French Quarter." Justin clicked on the link that took them to an article about a couple of kids finding a woman's body dumped behind a live oak in a court-yard near Canal. And from the description—a light-skinned black woman in a flowing white dress—Lucy knew this was the one she'd seen murdered in her dream.

"That's her. It has to be," she said, her eyes racing over the article.

A sudden sense of sorrow that she hadn't felt before filled her, maybe because until this very moment, part of her held out hope that for once her vision was skewed and that the victim had survived the attack. She closed her eyes and said a quick prayer for the poor woman.

"No clue to her identity," Justin said.

"That was yesterday. Maybe there's an update."

Justin checked the latest edition of the *Times-Picayune,* but to Lucy's disappointment, the dead woman's identity still hadn't been determined when the update had been written.

"Now what?" she asked.

"I have a feeling we're spinning our wheels here, but let me check other sources."

He typed in keywords—French Quarter, murder, courtyard—and got several sources to check. Unfortunately, none of these revealed the woman's identity, either.

"You don't think they're just holding the identity back until they contact the family or something?" Lucy asked.

"I doubt it. That's not the kind of information the police can suppress."

"What kind of information *can* they suppress?"

"We'll have to find out."

"One of your sources at the New Orleans Police Department?"

Justin nodded. "An old buddy of mine, Michael Hebert, was recently promoted to detective. He happens to work the French Quarter. We can go look for him right after we get some serious food."

Considering her stomach was demanding to be fed, Lucy wasn't about to argue with that idea. Besides, getting out of his apartment was a stellar idea considering the dreams she'd been having of the two of them in that bed upstairs.

AFTER THINKING ABOUT IT, Justin decided to call Mike and see if he could get him to meet them at Crescent City Oyster House for an early lunch.

The popular restaurant was just off Decatur Street and usually filled with tourists. They were seated right away, making Justin realize they were smart to have decided on an early lunch. The tables were mostly small, and half the place was taken up by a long counter where lone diners sat. The floors were well-worn pegged wood, the walls a dark burnished gold and hung with the work of local artists.

Mike had claimed he was too busy working on a case to go out for lunch, but Justin had guessed the case was the courtyard murder and had said he was pursuing it from a different angle. Mike had to be content with Justin's mysterious comment—he wouldn't say more—and Justin had to be content with Mike's promise to see what he could do about getting away long enough for a bite and an exchange of information.

In the meantime, Justin could concentrate on Lucy.

"So what's your pleasure, *chère?*" he asked, his own pleasure being the opportunity to make her blush.

She gave him a wide-eyed look over her menu. "What?"

"What are you thinking about…in the way of food, that is?"

He'd seen her staring at him when she thought he didn't notice. He'd noticed all right. She was interested but didn't want him to be aware of the fact. And he couldn't help but be curious why. What was making her shy away from the obvious attraction they shared?

"Give me a chance to get a good look at this menu and I'll decide."

Justin watched *her*. Not only was he familiar with the restaurant, he was equally familiar with the menu. He already knew what he would have. Though the menu was extensive, the restaurant was famous for the oysters that came in various guises.

"The raw oysters here are premium," Justin said, and solely to see Lucy's cheeks color continued, "and they have the added benefit of kicking up your libido a notch."

"My libido doesn't need to be kicked...or prodded or poked, for that matter...thank you very much."

"I've always appreciated a woman with a healthy libido," he murmured.

Lucy's cheeks filled with even more color, which she hid by lifting the menu higher. Justin grinned. He was liking her more and more.

"You don't need to hide behind your menu," he said softly. "Not from me."

She slapped her menu down on the table before looking around as if to assure herself they wouldn't be overheard. "I wouldn't if you would simply stop trying to torture me."

So she knew he was doing so on purpose. Justin

leaned in closer. "Are you tortured, Lucille? That means you're attracted to me."

"Hah."

"Hah?"

"Hah!"

"There's more than one way to find out." He reached across the table to touch her hand, and when she recoiled, he nodded and said, "Hah!" in triumph.

"I hate interrupting this interesting conversation," drawled a familiar smooth voice, "but I can only spare about ten minutes."

Justin looked up to see a man with brown hair spiked in every direction and blue eyes filled with amusement.

"Well, then, what are you waiting for?" Justin asked. "Pull up a chair. Lucy Ryan...Detective Mike Hebert."

Mike snagged a chair from a nearby table and shoved himself in between Justin and Lucy. The waitress arrived just then. Justin ordered a dozen raw oysters and a fried oyster platter, while Lucy ordered the obviously safer chicken gumbo. Mike ordered an oyster gumbo to go and asked that the waitress speed up things if she could.

Then Mike looked from Justin to Lucy. "So why are you investigating the courtyard murder? Does Ms. Ryan here have a personal interest?"

Justin evasively said, "We were hoping you could tell us something about the victim not reported in the media."

"And I was hoping you would tell me why her murder would interest you."

Mike was focusing on Lucy and Justin feared she would give herself away, so he said, "You know I cooperate with the NOPD any chance I get. But my saying anything now would be a little premature."

"Why don't you let me be the judge of that?"

"C'mon, Mike, you've trusted me with information before. And I've always come through with my promises."

"That's just it. You haven't made any promises."

"You give me a name and in seventy-two hours, I'll tell you everything I know."

"Twenty-four hours."

"Forty-eight."

If he didn't have a handle on what went down in two days, he would be glad to bring in the police. Though he would still play bodyguard to Lucy himself, of course.

Mike shrugged. "I can live with thirty-six."

Jumping in, Lucy said, "Great, that's settled then. So, what do you know about the victim that wasn't in the morning newspaper?"

Mike gave her an intense stare, as if trying to figure out her angle. Then he said, "That she was carrying a fancy tarot deck."

"Who in the French Quarter doesn't have a tarot deck," Lucy muttered. "Besides, all tarot cards are fancy."

"Not all of them are hand-painted, gold-leafed scenes from a bordello."

Lucy's eyebrows raised. "Really."

"Does that mean something to you?"

"Just that the deck sounds unusual, Detective. Were the cards signed by the artist?"

"Initials only—L.L."

"Lamar Landrieu."

"So I've been told."

Lucy grew thoughtful. "Considering he died some time ago, his already valuable work would be worth quite a bit."

Mike nodded. "But oddly enough, the victim wasn't dressed like she had a lot of money."

"I know—"

"How was she dressed?" Justin jumped in before Lucy could say that she'd *seen* the victim.

"In a simple, flowing white dress...as reported in the media."

Now Mike was glaring at *him* with suspicion, Justin realized. So he snapped his fingers and said, "Oh, yeah, now I remember reading that."

The waitress arrived with a brown bag and handed it and a check to Mike.

Justin reached over and took the check. "I'm buying," he told the waitress.

Nodding, she said, "Your order should be just a few more minutes."

"Why in such a hurry to leave that you can't even have a decent lunch?" Justin asked Mike. "Hot lead?"

"I wish. We're still trying to track down the source

of the tarot cards. Maybe whoever sold them will remember to whom. Do you have any idea of how many stores sell tarot decks in this city?''

"I imagine most of them," Justin said. "And then there's the Internet, of course." He couldn't let the detective go without asking. "Hey, Mike, about the Vaughn case—"

"Nothing new, sorry."

"Just thought I'd ask. Thanks, Mike. I owe you."

"And you'll be paying in exactly…" Mike checked his watch "…thirty-five hours and forty-nine minutes."

With that, Mike whistled some jazz tune and headed for the door.

Lucy waited until the detective was actually out of the restaurant before she asked, "Vaughn case?"

"Just something we were both working on before I went AWOL to bayou country," Justin said, not wanting to talk about it. Lucy never needed to know about Erica Vaughn. He turned the questioning back on her. "So what do you know about those cards that you didn't tell Mike?"

"Maybe nothing."

"Or maybe something?"

"I might have seen them before."

"Where?"

"In a shop called Taboo. The owner is a voodoo priestess—Odette LaFantary."

"You know her?"

"Only in the sense that we're both businesswomen and run into each other once in a while."

"Maybe that'll be enough for her to give you a name," Justin said.

Once they knew the identity of the dead woman, the rest should fall into place. Then he could call Mike and return the favor. Whether or not Lucy liked it, though, he would stick to her like glue until the murderer was in custody.

And after that?

Justin didn't want to go there just yet. No premature conclusions. He didn't want to make another mistake. Didn't want another client killed. Not that Lucy was a client. Not exactly.

One step at a time....

TABOO WAS LOCATED in a busy part of the French Quarter, just down the block from Lucy and Dana's Bal Masque. A couple of giggling tourists came out of the shop just as Lucy led Justin inside where exotic scents assaulted them.

Dressed in a loose red and gold caftan—the same colors that decorated the rear of the store which was devoted to voodoo, Odette, the self-styled priestess looked up from the makeup counter she was rearranging. Her expression briefly reflected her recognition of Lucy before it morphed into something neutral.

"How may I help you?" Odette asked.

Snaking an arm around Lucy's waist and pulling her close before she could protest, Justin said, "My lady and I need a love potion."

What in the heck did he think he was doing? And not only with the request—he was getting awfully familiar with that hand. She could feel each of his fingers as they pressed into her flesh just below the healing wound.

"Love potion?" Odette echoed. "For the two of you?"

"That's right."

"Usually one buys a love potion when one wants another to fall in love with him. Or her. The two of you don't seem to need that kind of help."

Lucy was mortified. She might be in lust with Justin, but certainly not in love, and even so, she didn't want someone who was nearly a complete stranger to read that off her. Yikes—was she that transparent?

"You don't understand," Justin said, lowering his voice. "We want a lo-o-ove potion. You know, something for a really special night. Something…exotic."

Lucy felt heat creep up her neck and go straight for her ears. Great. He'd gone and made it worse. She was so chagrined she couldn't utter a word even if she could think of something to say.

"A-a-ah, now I understand," Odette said with a knowing smile.

Justin asked, "So can you help us?"

"Of course."

Odette turned her back to get something and Lucy glared up at Justin. In response, he grinned and leaned down for a kiss. Lucy wanted to smack him, then, but she didn't want to give Odette a show. So she kissed Justin back and hoped he was as hot and bothered as he was making her.

It would serve him right!

Suddenly, Justin let her go, his expression hungry. Lucy turned her back on him and watched Odette set a vial in a holder and pull several mysterious bottles from a cabinet.

"While you're making up our potion," Justin said, "we'll look around."

"Please do so."

Justin pulled Lucy away from the makeup and scents. Several yards away, they entered voodoo territory and a display of tarot cards.

Lucy leaned into Justin and whispered, "What are you thinking?"

"That she'll be more likely to answer questions if she's made a sale."

"You couldn't just ask for one of her scents? Or some bubble bath?"

"That wouldn't have gotten the desired results."

And what were the desired results? Lucy suspected they had to do more with her than with answers.

Vowing vengeance—why should she be the only one embarrassed?—Lucy took a good look at the tarot display, especially those under glass—the more valuable decks—but didn't see any work by Lamar Landrieu.

Wiggling free of Justin, she made her way back to Odette and in a whisper loud enough for him to hear, said, "Can you add something to..." She indicated him. "...you know, make him more...potent?"

Odette's eyebrows shot up, but she said, "Of course. Then I'll split the potion in two and mark the vial with male and female symbols. Just don't get them mixed up.''

Lucy smiled as she glanced back at Justin and savored his glower for a moment. Then she watched Odette cork the first vial and use a marker to draw a symbol that indicated this one was for her.

"You know, the last time I was in your shop, I saw a tarot deck that I really loved, but it seems to be gone.''

"Which one?" Odette asked, turning back to the cabinet and removing another vial.

"The bordello deck hand-painted by Lamar Landrieu.''

"Oh, I just sold that deck a few days ago.''

"Will you be getting another like it?''

Adding a dash of the extra ingredient to the remaining vial, Odette said, "I'm afraid it was one of a kind.''

"Darn. And I really wanted to buy it.'' Lucy lowered her voice. "In case you didn't guess, my boyfriend is kind of…well, you know…kinky.'' Chalk up two for her. "That deck would have done it for him. Maybe if you contacted the person who bought the deck from you…?''

"I doubt that she would want to sell it.'' Odette corked the second vial. "She reads tarot professionally and said this deck was exactly what she needed for a particular and important client.''

"Well, maybe she could at least read Justin's tarot. Where can we find her?''

"Jackson Square.''

"Oh, great. We can go right over there. Wait a minute—what's her name?"

Odette thought about it for a moment. "Sophie. I don't remember her last name."

"I'm sure we'll find her. I mean, how many tarot-reading Sophies can there be at Jackson Square?"

Odette marked the second vial with the male symbol. "All done. That'll be a hundred dollars."

"A hundred..." Justin cleared his throat and pulled out his wallet, muttering, "No problem."

Odette smiled serenely as she said, "Viagra would have been cheaper, but you wouldn't have gotten the information you came for."

8

"WE REALLY PUT ONE OVER ON HER," Justin said caustically, as they left Taboo a few minutes later.

"Odette LaFantaray is a well-known voodoo priestess," Lucy reminded him. "Who knows what kind of powers she has. She probably read your mind."

"Or she's simply good at reading people in general." A requirement for those going into one of the mystic trades so prevalent in New Orleans, he thought.

"Or that."

Justin dropped his sunglasses in place over the bridge of his nose. The afternoon was hot and humid and the sun shone at full force. Despite the discomfort of the weather, the streets and restaurants and shops were crowded with people seemingly happy to fry their brains in pursuit of pleasure. High tourist season brought large crowds to the French Quarter. Just about any season did, especially on the weekends. But summers were especially crowded.

Tourists apparently didn't care that their bodies were dripping with sweat…as if they'd just engaged in a round of hot, sweaty sex.

That thought occurred to Justin when a couple in a doorway caught his attention. They were locked in a hot embrace, rubbing against each other, and the man's hand had mysteriously disappeared behind the woman....

Still smarting at Lucy's implication to Odette that he needed some kind of help to get it up—he was certainly having no trouble at the moment—Justin said, "By the way, remind me never to cross you."

"You mean again," she said.

Her grin and wiggled eyebrows set his heart racing and his erection throbbing. What was it about her that had him in such a spin? Maybe it was the pure part of her, the part that had made her try to save someone she hadn't even known, that appealed to him most.

Good thing he had a modicum of self-control, Justin thought, or he just might pull Lucy into one of those doorways to see how far she would let *him* go in public.

"You just didn't seem like a woman who focuses on revenge," he said in mock complaint.

"Normally I'm not, but I decided to make an exception for you."

"Thanks a lot."

"You're welcome," Lucy said airily. "Not to change the subject, but do you mind if we stop by Bal Masque so I can check in with Dana before going on to Jackson Square?"

"Fine by me."

Justin wanted to know everything he could about Lucy Ryan, whether personal or business. Not that he thought working with her to find a murderer was going to come back to bite him. It wasn't that, at all.

Rather, he was not only attracted to her, but he liked her and wanted to spend some quality time with her. True, mostly he wanted to explore the various positions such a thing as a love potion would instigate, but after the case was solved.

He couldn't remember the last time he'd felt that focused on any woman.

As they reached the cross-street, Lucy said, "Our shop is right around the corner."

And a moment later, Justin followed her inside Bal Masque. The shop was a single storefront wide, but it was two rooms deep, the front filled with product, the rear with long tables where customers were making their own masks.

"I'll be just a minute," Lucy said. "Look around. Make yourself at home."

Justin watched Lucy saunter to the register where Dana was taking care of a customer. He couldn't keep his eyes off her. The way she moved with such grace, swinging her hips so unselfconsciously, was enough to give him another hard-on.

To take his mind off his dick, he checked out the masks mounted on the walls—from expensive Mardi Gras masks to very expensive pieces of art not meant to be worn. He saw little that reminded him of the masks in Lucy's living room, however, and wondered if that meant they sold faster than she could produce them or that she was simply too modest to make a big deal over her own designs.

The bell over the door tinkled and he glanced back to see a young woman dressed in black enter. Obviously a Goth, she appeared to be ready for Mardi Gras even now. Her hair was a dark, blood-red against pale skin whitened with makeup. Her black-ringed eyes stood out, too, as did her dark red lips.

He wondered at her coming into a mask shop when she was already wearing one.

But it seemed that Lucy and Dana knew the young woman. The Goth and Lucy hugged each other. Justin couldn't hear what they were saying.

Curious—was this an art school friend?—he made his way toward the front counter, passing tables and shelves filled with the more usual tourist fare—souvenirs in the form of inexpensive sequined and feathered masks, silk-screened Mardi Gras T-shirts and baskets of mask key chains and pencils. Something for every budget.

"Oh, Justin," Lucy said, rolling her eyes at him in some kind of warning. "This is my sister Jennifer."

"Call me Jenn," the overly made-up woman said. "So Justin, it seems that you've been keeping my big sister busy the last few days."

"I've done my best," he said and tried to look past the makeup to find a resemblance between the sisters. Impossible. The Goth disguise was complete.

"What have you two been up to?" Jenn's raccoon eyes targeted the bag in his hand.

Justin couldn't help himself. He held up the package from Taboo. "Love potion," was all he said before looking for Lucy's reaction.

Her blushes were charming, but this one especially so. Her reaction made him want to take her somewhere private so they could try out Odette's potion and see if it worked.

"Hmm, seems like there's a lot you've been keeping to yourself lately, Lucy," Jenn said, wide-eyed as she studied her sister.

"We're new," Justin volunteered. "Lucy doesn't trust the relationship. Give her time and you won't be able to stop her from talking."

"That sounds more like our Lucy," Dana said with a laugh.

"We need to get going," the object of discussion said, marching toward the door.

"Don't worry, I'll hold down the fort," Dana assured her. "But you'd better be here on the weekend or I won't be responsible for the carnage."

Lucy simply waved a hand at her partner without turning to look at her.

And Justin followed her straight out the door. "Whoa, *chère*, wait up."

"No, you keep up."

"You're not angry with me, are you?"

Justin worried that he might have gone too far teasing Lucy in front of her sister and best friend. She was focused on getting to Jackson Square and didn't spare him so much as a glance. Her spine was straight, her shoulders stiff. Definitely angry. Not having a better idea of how to cool her down, he hoped engaging her in conversation might get her mind off her irritation with him.

"So, how did your sister get herself into the Goth-culture thing?"

Lucy sighed and slowed a bit. "Jenn is complicated. She majored in theater and believes in living her art."

"She's in some Goth play?"

"Lingerie. She's modeling a line of Goth lingerie, kind of like a spokesperson for them. Not that she actually speaks much. At least not when she's being photographed."

"Unusual job."

"Not for Jenn. You wouldn't believe some of the stories. Once she played a pregnant woman in a play and felt the need to wear the pregnancy gear 24/7."

"Must have been difficult taking a shower," an amused Justin said.

"And then there was the time she modeled at a motorcycle convention. She lived in leather for months afterward."

"Be thankful she didn't buy a hog."

"Who says? The downpayment was more than she made on the whole job. She wasn't a good rider, though. Three falls and she sold the thing."

Not knowing if Lucy would be insulted if he laughed, Justin kept his amusement under control, saying, "At least she learned something from the experience."

"Really? That's why she decided to try out for Cirque du Soleil and signed up for private gymnast lessons."

Feeling like the straight man in a George Burns–Gracie Allen routine, Justin asked, "And how did that go?"

"Well, it ended with Jenn's arm in a cast," Lucy

admitted. "And she can't figure out why no man wants to see her more than a few times."

Personally, Justin pitied the poor bastard who would get involved with such a kook. Not that he would ever put that thought in words to Lucy. Knowing her even for such a short time, he was certain that if someone else criticized her sister, that someone would have his ears boxed.

A titillating thought if that someone were Lucy. He imagined her coming at him, her expression serious...until he touched her, that was. He would do a lot of touching in a lot of special places. He would use that love potion on her. Then she would forget what it was she was angry about.

He fantasized for a moment, imagining her in his bed and him trailing a stream of scented oil from her breasts to her belly to the vee between her thighs. She would sigh and arch and open for him, and he would spread the liquid gold along the heart of her. She would writhe under his touch. The potion would make her burn for him and it would take him all night to satiate her....

Realizing Jackson Square was just ahead, Justin ignored the hard on he'd given himself as he switched into private investigator mode. No more joking around here. No more fantasies. Not if he wanted to get a handle on this case before his thirty-six hours were up.

"SO WHERE DO WE START?" Lucy asked, feeling strange vibes coming from Justin as they arrived at the heart of the city.

Jackson Square was a beautifully landscaped park once known as Plaze d'Armas, the site of public executions and military exercises. Today, it evoked romance, and was a source of big tourist dollars. She eyed Justin from beneath her lashes and wished romance could be uppermost on their minds, even if for a little while.

"Why don't we split up and start asking if anyone knows a tarot reader named Sophie," Justin suggested. "Probably best not to say why we're asking."

"Okay. Here goes."

Lucy surveyed the entrepreneurs lined up across from the cathedral...the collection of shops and restaurants below the Pontalba Apartments...Café du Monde.

The sights and sounds and smells of this area were distinctly New Orleans. Color and jazz and spice, she thought. The flagstone walkway was home to artists and tap dancers and mimes and jugglers in addition to those who claimed to be mystics. Around one corner, jazz musicians performed, and around the other, a whole lineup of horse and mule-drawn carriages awaited the tourist trade.

If only she and Justin could be sharing all this, holding hands and strolling through the crown like lovers....

Images from her dreams crowded Lucy's mind and it took all her effort to concentrate.

She approached a woman who'd set up a card table amidst the artists' easels. A sign indicated this was Madame Rouge, and indeed the well-endowed woman was wearing a vibrant red dress and head covering that set off her dark skin.

"Sit, child."

How in the world did she deal cards with those two inch nails? Lucy thought as she slid into the chair, saying, "I'm looking for a tarot reader named Sophie."

"What you think I am, huh?" Madame Rouge asked indignantly. "The best tarot reader not only in Jackson Square, but in all New Orleans." The woman flicked her nails at Lucy. "Shoo! I have time only for paying customers."

Lucy rose and started to leave, then hesitated. "Look, I can pay you whatever you charge for the information."

The indignant tarot reader shook her head and turned her attention to two teenaged girls who were obviously interested in having her read *their* cards.

Well, that didn't exactly go as expected.

Lucy looked around for Justin and saw him across from the Cabildo talking to a musician carrying a sax. The musician was shaking his head. It didn't look like Justin was having any luck, either.

Again she wished they could be together. She had a hard time keeping her eyes off him and on the performers who roamed up and down the street. Maybe one of them had known Sophie. She waited until a juggler dressed as a pirate caught all his pins, then she approached him, saying, "Excuse me, but I'm looking for someone—"

His swarthy face broke into a leer. "I'm all yours,

chère, as soon as I'm done here for the day.'' He took a bow as tourists dropped money into his pirate hat.

"You don't understand. I'm looking for a woman—"

"A ménage à trois?" A snaky smile curled his lips. "Oh, la, I wish I could help you there."

"Look, I'm not interested in sex. I'm…"

But before Lucy could tell him she was looking for Sophie, his dark eyebrows shot up and he gave her a look of pity and clucked to himself. Then he turned his back on her and went on with his routine for a new group of tourists.

Chagrined, Lucy backed off. Great. Two strikes out of two.

She scanned her choices—mostly artists whose work was displayed attached to the black iron fencing that circled the park. None of them admitted to knowing a Sophie who read Tarot at Jackson Square.

Thoroughly frustrated, Lucy looked again for Justin, but now he seemed to have disappeared. Perhaps he was having more luck than she.

Lucy certainly hoped so. She felt a responsibility—a burden, even—to find the murderer.

Why else would she have had the dream?

The hair on the back of Lucy's neck suddenly stood at attention. Though no one was directly behind her, she felt as if someone were breathing on her.

She turned to see a light-skinned black man wearing a Saints T-shirt, his hair in short dreadlocks, staring at her from his table several yards away. His sign identified him as Emile Poree, Guide to the Future. Raising one hand, he waved for her to come over to him.

Lucy's senses all twitched. Chances were this guy would come on to her just as the juggler had. And yet…she found her feet moving without being conscious of making that decision.

"Mr. Poree, I'm not a tourist," she told him right off.

"But you need a spiritual guide. Sit."

"Spiritual guide? Not exactly," she said carefully.

But something compelled Lucy to sit anyway and when she placed her hands on the table, he covered her right hand with his left. The gesture wasn't intimate and yet an indescribable energy went through her at his touch. Startled, she felt her pulse surge. What the heck was going on here?

Gazing into her eyes, he said, "You've lost something and need to find it."

"Not exactly. I'm looking for someone." The way he studied her made her nerves jangle. "Her name is Sophie. She's a tarot reader who works this area."

His gaze intensified. "I believe you mean Sophie Delacorte."

"When was the last time you saw her?"

He turned her hand, brushed her palm with his fingertips and studied it for a moment. "You're not a policewoman."

"No, I'm not. Call me an interested party."

Emile's gaze met hers and slowly he nodded. "I sense that. But why?"

"You tell me."

"Something you saw disturbed you. Something powerful." He cocked his head and then nodded. "You have the sight."

"Again, not exactly."

"However you describe your gift doesn't matter. What matters is what you do with it."

He was guessing. He had to be. But how? Why would he go there?

Then she remembered the energy she'd felt at his touch. A familiar energy. When they'd been young, she'd gotten that kind of energy off Jenn. And Jenn too had often known about something before it happened to her.

What if Emile were a real clairvoyant, not one of the charlatans working the tourists? He was obviously different. No costume. No props. Just him.

And he apparently had recognized her as a like soul.

Was that connection enough?

Lucy didn't know if Emile could or would tell her more, but it was worth a shot.

"Can we talk away from here later?" she asked, thinking he might at least know something more about Sophie Delacorte that would help them. "Just to be clear, this isn't a come-on and I won't be alone."

"Another interested party?"

"Right. He is." She emphasized the *he*.

"I can spare enough time for a café au lait." Emile checked his watch. "Café du Monde in fifteen minutes."

"We'll be there. My name is Lucy Ryan, by the way. How much do I owe you?"

He shook his head and made a dismissive gesture. Lucy stood and started to move away, but then she stopped and tried to impress upon him the importance of his carrying through with the promise.

"This is a matter of life or death, Emile."

He shrugged as if she wasn't telling him something that he didn't already know. "Yes, Lucy. Yours."

That unnerved Lucy enough to make her hurry away from Emile, needing to quickly find one reality-based private eye.

9

WHAT THE HELL kind of private investigator was he? Justin wondered, when he couldn't get something as simple as a last name from one of the people he'd questioned.

He was having no luck at all. And he was beginning to wonder if they'd too easily taken Odette at her word when he saw Lucy round the corner wearing an intent expression like she'd learned something that he hadn't.

And then she saw him and her expression changed to one of relief and something else. Something soft and alluring. Something that made Justin's heart beat harder and his feet move faster to get to her. With the sun making her red hair glow and an inviting smile lighting up her freckled face, she was irresistible.

"What is it?" he asked. "Did you find someone who knows her?"

"Knew her," Lucy corrected him. "Though he may or may not know that she's dead."

"Focus, Lucy, focus."

Lucy rolled her eyes and said, "The woman's name is Sophie Delacorte. The psychic who told me that agreed to meet us at Café du Monde in fifteen minutes, hopefully to give us further information. Make that about ten minutes now.''

''A psychic?''

''Named Emile Poree. And don't poo-poo what you don't understand,'' she said, sounding a little tense.

Everyone knew the supposed clairvoyants around Jackson Square were simply working a trade. Somehow, he figured Lucy didn't want to hear that—she had her own psychic dreams, after all—and so he decided not to voice that opinion.

Instead, Justin simply asked, ''You think this Emile Poree will show?''

''I'm counting on it.''

''Let's get over there and get a table, then.''

They cut through the heart of Jackson Square with its statue of General Andrew Jackson mounted on his horse. The park was laid out in a sun pattern, and oak-shaded walkways streamed out from the center like rays. People gathered on the benches—some alone, but mostly couples.

Justin thought it was a park for lovers. The French Quarter was a neighborhood for lovers. New Orleans was a city for lovers. Even as he thought it, Justin let his gaze drift to Lucy, and he couldn't help but hunger for her.

Exiting the park, they waited for traffic to stop before crossing to the outdoor café where the patrons people-watched while enjoying café au lait and beignets, a French Quarter tradition.

Though the place was crowded, Justin was relieved

to see an empty table at the back where they would be able to talk with some privacy.

They were barely seated when Lucy said, "There he is now, waiting to cross the street."

Justin got a look at the supposed psychic—not what he'd expected. A Saints T-shirt and jeans wasn't exactly the costume de rigueur. So Emile Poree wasn't trying to make a big production of himself to the tourists.

A waitress arrived at their table, pad in hand. "What can I get you?"

"Café au lait for three."

Emile arrived at the table just as the waitress hurried off.

Standing, Justin held out his hand. "Justin Guidry, private investigator."

Emile held on to him a second longer than made Justin comfortable. "I'm sorry."

"That I'm a P.I.?"

"For whatever happened to make you so unsettled."

Justin got the idea Emile didn't mean Sophie Delacorte's death, yet he said, "Murder always unsettles me."

They sat and Emile asked, "What is your interest in Sophie Delacorte?"

"You heard about the body of the woman found in the courtyard, right?" Lucy asked.

Emile appeared shocked. "That's why Sophie hasn't been around the square?" He mumbled something under his breath in the local patois that sounded like a prayer. "You're certain you have the right woman?"

"The police haven't identified her yet," Justin admitted, "but we've been doing some digging ourselves. What didn't appear in the media is something she had on her person. A particular valuable tarot deck that Lucy had seen in a shop. The shop owner said she sold it to a tarot reader named Sophie who worked Jackson Square. So here we are."

Emile nodded. "And there was only one Sophie and no one has seen her for the past few days, so she must be the one. But you still haven't answered my question." He turned to Lucy when he again asked, "What is *your* interest in this?"

She licked her lips and softly said, "I saw it…the murder."

Just then the waitress arrived with their chicory-laced coffee and hot milk. Justin pulled a ten-dollar bill out of his wallet, and not wanting another interruption, told her to keep the change.

"Thanks," the waitress said. "You want anything else, you just signal."

The moment she was gone, Emile leaned in across the table and in a low voice said to Lucy, "You weren't actually present when she died, were you?"

"No."

He nodded as if satisfied. "I felt the power when I touched your hand. You had a vision, yes?"

"A dream," Lucy said. "I went to the courtyard, hoping I could stop the tragedy from happening. I was too late."

"But now *your* life is in danger…so the murderer must have seen you."

Lucy nodded.

She wore her fear openly for a moment, and Justin wanted to take her in his arms and tell her it would be all right. That he wouldn't let anything happen to her. But how could he guarantee her that?

Emile reached out and touched Lucy's hand. Justin stiffened until he realized this wasn't an intimate touch. The psychic was using the contact to somehow connect with Lucy in a way he couldn't fathom. He imagined he could feel the air around them change, as if the atmosphere wan suddenly charged with power.

Or maybe it was simply his imagination.

Then Emile leaned back and nodded. "I believe you are a good person, Lucy Ryan, or you wouldn't have tried to save poor Sophie. She might not have been the most honest of women, but she had a good heart."

"Not the most honest of women?" Justin echoed. Did he mean she'd said whatever it took to please her clients to make a living, or was there was more to it? "What kind of scam was she into?"

Emile merely said, "She never talked about her business opportunities, but even so, I don't want to see her murderer get away with this. So how can I help you?"

An unsatisfactory answer, but Justin wasn't going to push. Emile Poree was the only direct link they had to the murder victim, so he would have to handle the man with kid gloves. Something told him that Sophie had been killed because she'd tried to swindle the wrong client.

The question was: who?

RELIEVED THAT EMILE was obviously willing to tell them what he knew about Sophie, Lucy said, "The tarot deck found on her body...supposedly she bought it for a particular client. Do you know who that might be?"

"What did this tarot deck look like?"

"You're psychic," Justin said. "You tell us."

Emile laughed and shook his head. "A nonbeliever. How did you get hooked up with this one, Lucy?"

"He saved my life. And I wouldn't exactly call Justin a nonbeliever. More like a skeptic."

"Does this skeptic know that we don't control our gifts but that they control us?"

"Hello, skeptic sitting right here," Justin said, apparently feeling left out.

Lucy ignored him. "I've tried to explain that to him, but that's the problem with skeptics—they don't always retain what they're told."

"All right, knock off the wit," Justin said, his voice raised slightly. "Murder is serious business!"

Realizing he'd just gotten the notice of several people nearby, Lucy kicked him under the table and hissed, "Justin, please! It's just a game, okay."

"What?"

She felt eyes aimed their way and was desperate to be free of the unwanted attention.

"I know you love that stupid board game," she

said, "but who cares if it was the butler in the study with a lampshade or what. You won and that's all that counts."

The curious eyes returned to other things, and Lucy sagged with relief. Justin was looking at her as if he'd never seen her before and Emile was sitting back, smiling, seemingly enjoying the show.

"Keep your voice down," she murmured. "We don't need an audience. Now where were we?"

"The tarot deck," Emile said. "You were going to tell me what it looked like."

"You don't need a description," Justin said. "Just tell us about Sophie's clients."

Justin gave her a look that probably meant she was supposed to keep the details to herself, Lucy thought. For some reason, he didn't want the description getting out. Lucy didn't see what it could hurt, but Justin was better at this than she, so she would let him take the lead.

"Sophie had swarms of clients every day she worked," Emile said. "The tourists are as thick as flies right now and she was very popular."

"What about the regulars?"

"There were a few. An old woman who wanted to know about the afterlife. A teenager who was looking for reassurances about her boyfriend. And then there was the gambler who kept wanting to know when his luck was going to turn. No one who looked to be any kind of threat, though."

"What about private clients away from the square?" Justin pressed. "She must have had some."

"Of course. But like I told you, Sophie Delacorte didn't talk about those opportunities. And the only time I ever saw her away from Jackson Square was by accident. It was in a club near Esplanade—a place called Music of the Night. Sophie said she lived nearby."

"Nothing more specific?"

"Afraid not. Sorry."

"At the club," Justin said, "did you see her talking with anyone?"

Emile nodded. "Another woman. A tall blonde named Erica."

Lucy was aware that Justin's tone changed subtly when he asked, "No last name?"

"If she told me, I don't remember."

"What did she look like, other than being tall and blond?"

"Beautiful and rich. Designer outfit. And she wore this ring on her middle finger that was so big, I wondered how she could wave that hand so easily when she called the bartender over for another drink."

"Lots of diamonds, huh?" Lucy asked.

"No. A giant topaz and lots of gold studded with emeralds and rubies. An incredible design. Asian, I think. But it was a one-of-a-kind ring."

"One of a kind," Justin echoed, drawing back from the table.

"Maybe someone at the club can give you her last name," Emile said.

Realizing Justin wasn't paying attention, his mind

clearly in other things, Lucy asked, "Was this Erica one of Sophie's clients?"

"Truthfully? I couldn't say."

"Anyone who could tell us more?"

"Maybe the bartender who was waiting on them. A good-looking Creole boy named Zeke Montplaisir."

"Anything else you can tell us, Emile?" Justin asked.

Apparently, he was back on the case, Lucy thought, wondering what he had been thinking about.

"About Sophie?" Emile asked. "Or Erica?"

"Sophie," Justin said without hesitating.

But Lucy had the oddest feeling that he was lying. That he was more interested in the mysterious and rich Erica than he was in the murder victim.

Why?

Emile couldn't tell them anything more, but he asked to be kept informed and volunteered to help in the investigation if he could. Justin suggested he might be called in to identify Sophie's body. He and Justin exchanged business cards.

"As for you, Lucy Ryan," Emile said, his expression intent, "you need to learn to use your gift to your best advantage."

"I am doing the best I can."

"I don't sense that is so. Right now, you're a channel. Learn to be more."

With that, he left, leaving Lucy confused. Emile had said that their gifts controlled them—now he was indicating the reverse.

So which was it?

Was it even possible to be more than a receiver of her dreams? She'd tried changing the outcome more than once to no avail. But she'd never tried manipulating her gift to give her information.

If Emile was serious, then maybe it was possible to do more, and so, learn the identity of the man who'd murdered Sophie Delacorte.

"WHAT'S GOING ON WITH YOU?" Lucy asked Justin when they got back to his apartment.

"What do you mean?"

"You're quiet. Withdrawn."

He'd been this way since Emile had mentioned the blonde named Erica. They'd left Café du Monde shortly after the psychic and had headed for Music of the Night only to find that the nightclub was indeed that and didn't even open until nine. They'd had a fast dinner before coming back to Justin's loft to wait—not that Justin had eaten half of his food. He'd played with the rest, pushing it around to the edges of his plate like she had when she'd been a child and had wanted to "hide" the vegetables she didn't like. Throughout all that, Justin had been less than fully present.

"Sorry," he muttered, opening the refrigerator door and burying his head inside as if he was hungry now. "I always get distracted thinking about a case. Want something to drink?" he asked, pulling out a can.

"No, thanks. Funny, but I didn't notice you were distracted until Emile mentioned the blonde." Lucy waited for Justin to deny it, but he didn't. "So what's with this Erica?'' Was the woman an ex of some kind? Ex-girlfriend? Ex-wife? "What does she mean to you?''

He popped the top on a root beer and took a long slug, then said, "If it's who I think it is, then we're talking about the biggest failure of my life."

So she'd been right, Lucy realized gloomily. She plopped herself on a stool by the breakfast bar. Justin was probably still in love with this Erica. Though why it should matter to her didn't compute. She might be attracted to him—and he might haunt her dreams—but she wasn't about to act on any of it.

Even though Justin *had* put himself in the middle of this case, she was convinced that as long as they weren't lovers, he would come out of this investigation alive. Realizing she felt unsettled anyway, Lucy wondered if it was because of the danger...or because of Erica.

"You know, sometimes things are simply not meant to be," she said, thinking both about the end of his relationship with the mystery woman and about the impossibility of his starting one with her.

"Meant to be?" Justin frowned and insisted, "Erica Vaughn was a client."

Feeling suddenly lighter inside, Lucy asked, "Vaughn? Where have I heard that...the detective...you asked him about the Vaughn case."

"Yeah, because it was one I blew."

"That happens. We all make mistakes."

"But not ones that get someone else killed."

"What?"

"That's my bayou secret, Lucy," he said, rounding the counter and stopping in front of her. "The reason I was hiding out at the fishing camp. I didn't know if I was ever coming back to New Orleans until you came along."

"What happened?"

"Erica Vaughn hired me to find her younger sister Theresa. The girl had been having an affair with an important man. Well, that according to Theresa. Who knows what important means to an eighteen-year-old. Erica didn't know who the man was, but she did know that he was married. She tried getting more from her sister, but Theresa grew hostile. And then she disappeared. She was legally an adult, and there was no evidence of foul play. The police didn't act on it, especially not after getting the married man angle."

"So Erica decided to investigate on her own."

"To have me investigate," Justin clarified. "Or that's the way it was supposed to be. I got a few leads, but quickly ran into a dead end. And then Erica's body was found along the Moonwalk. The official story is that she was out taking a late stroll when she was mugged. Something went wrong…maybe she struggled…and she ended up dead. Knifed to death."

"Knifed? Like Sophie," Lucy murmured.

"Like Sophie," he echoed. "Both women were alone at night in fairly deserted areas. Both women were knifed to death. Both were thought to be victims of muggers. And now I find they knew each other."

"You think—"

"That they were killed by the same man? That's exactly what I've been thinking."

If that was truth, that explained why her psychic dreams had brought them together. One man responsible for both deaths. And possibly a third, Lucy thought, remembering the younger sister Theresa, who apparently was still missing.

To her mind, this was no coincidence. It was proof that she and Justin were destined to find the killer together.

"I'm such a hell of a private investigator," he muttered, "that I had to be hit over the head before seeing the similarities between their deaths."

"But you didn't know Erica and Sophie were connected in any way."

"But I should have been the one to make the connection," he insisted.

Justin's expression grew dark once more and it was obvious that he was turning in on himself. Lucy imagined the pain he must have felt when Erica Vaughn's body had been found.

The guilt…

"You can't blame yourself," she said gently.

"I can. And I do."

Feeling his agony, Lucy leaned forward on her stool so she could wrap her arms around Justin and she nestled her forehead against his collarbone. The gesture was meant to comfort him, and perhaps for a moment it did.

Then heat began to penetrate her. The heat of his

body. The way he stirred against her, she guessed their closeness was affecting him in exactly the same way.

"Oh, Lu-u-cille," Justin murmured, as he caught her mouth in a sweet, savage kiss.

Part of her knew this was wrong. That she should back off before they got caught in something they couldn't stop. Before she did something irreversible, something that would get him killed.

But another part of her couldn't help herself. One kiss, she thought. Just one kiss. Surely that couldn't hurt. Surely that was making her feel good, better than she ever remembered feeling before.

She couldn't stop, not now, not while his tongue plunged deep inside her mouth, the rhythm making her think of him plunging deep inside her.

He swept his hands over her breasts and it was all she could do not to jump him. Her nipples hardened and the soft flesh ached for more. The ache spread outward and lower—especially lower to her most tender flesh—and she wondered if just one kiss wasn't just one big, fat mistake.

Before she could end it, he pulled her out of the chair and up against the length of his body. And then she felt him, hard and long, throbbing through their clothing against her leg. Hands cradling her bottom, he repositioned her before him so his erection pressed low against her belly. Oh, the sensations that spread through her like wildfire! Her hips moved of their own volition so that she could touch him to her center, and she wanted more than anything to rid them both of all garments so she could feel him deep inside her.

Closing her eyes, she could imagine it—her straddling him, dancing her bottom over his belly and thighs, teasing his cock with her wet flesh, then plunging down its length.

She moaned and he swallowed the sound as if he were having the same fantasy.

As if he'd had the same dreams.

Dreams!

Good grief, what in the world was she thinking? This was supposed to be just a kiss, not a prelude to the world's best sex!

Lucy slid her palms against Justin's chest, and pushed at him. He didn't give over easily, though, and allowed her no more than a little breathing room.

"What's wrong?" he whispered in a sexy voice.

She looked into those bedroom eyes, and knew exactly what he wanted. It was what she wanted, as well. It was what they couldn't have, at least now. Maybe someday, after the killer was behind bars, maybe then.

In the meantime, she couldn't tell him the truth, couldn't admit she'd seen him shot because of her.

Feeling bad at having to do this, she murmured in return, "We're allowing ourselves to be distracted."

"We deserve a distraction."

"But not at the expense of our concentration. Erica and Sophie deserve to have their killer caught. By us. We owe it to them."

Lucy figured her sounding so reasonable was what made Justin back off. But then his expression closed as if she'd shamed him. Now she felt worse.

"You're right, of course." He checked his watch.

"We have some time. Maybe I'll go online, see if anything new has happened in the Vaughn case since I've been gone."

"Sure. And I have a couple of calls to make. If you don't mind, that is."

"Not a bit."

Now they were playing at being polite strangers, Lucy thought, hating the pretense. Her body was screaming at her, telling her that she was an idiot, that she should take pleasure while she had the opportunity.

But the opportunity was already missed. Justin had already turned his back on her and was at his computer. Not knowing what else to do, Lucy climbed the steps up to the loft bedroom where she could make those calls in privacy.

But to do so, she had to lie across his bed. *The* bed. The one in her dreams.

Nope. She wasn't going there. Instead, she hunkered down on the floor and made her first call.

IF THEY DIDN'T get Lucy Ryan and permanently shut her mouth soon, not only would his career be ended, but he would see the inside of a cell at the very least. He didn't intend for that to happen. He'd never intended to commit multiple murders in the first place, but what was done was done. He couldn't go back and change things now.

It was all that little bitch Theresa Vaughn's fault.

He stared at his bodyguards. They both stood there, unable to face him. Walter was checking his nails, while Phil was wiping some invisible speck of dirt off his damn shoe.

"What do you mean, you can't find her?" he demanded, trying to keep his blood pressure from rising sky-high. "I got you the name and address that goes with the license plate number, didn't I? Do I need to draw you a map?"

"We found the place, boss," Phil said. "I'm telling you, she took a powder."

Walter added, "She was gone when we got there. Her roommate, too."

So they'd just given up and come back here to report to him. He poured himself a bourbon and tossed it back. The liquor burned its way into his gut, calming him some.

"Did it occur to you that she might return?" he asked, trying like hell to keep his voice reasonable.

His bodyguards looked at each other and shrugged.

"Well, why am I surprised?" he muttered to himself. "I want that place watched 24/7, do you understand? One of you is to be on it at all times."

"Sure thing, boss," Phil said. "We're gonna be right on it now."

"Good. Don't let her slip through her fingers again or—"

"Or what?" Walter asked with a glimmer in his eyes that looked like a counterthreat.

"Or we'll all suffer the consequences," he said. "We were seen together, so we'll all be held responsible. Don't forget that."

It wouldn't do to rile Walter, especially. He had a

vicious temper. Plus, he needed them to cooperate, to help him find Lucy Ryan.

He needed them to finish her off.

He wouldn't rest until they did.

10

ZEKE MONTPLAISIR was indeed a good-looking Creole boy, just as Emile had described the bartender at Music of the Night. Heck, Zeke was probably the prettiest thing going in the place with his perfect café-au-lait skin, a burnished buzz cut and smoky eyes.

Lucy took a long look around the club.

There seemed to be as many threesomes as couples, and they weren't simply engaged in talk. Sitting with her back to the bar, Lucy watched a woman who was dancing between two men. The one in front seemed to be plunging his tongue down her throat and not-too-subtly cupping her breasts, while the one behind her was pressing up against her bottom so intimately he might as well be...

Then she realized they were imitating a scantily clad threesome dancing on the other side of the room.

Actually, a lot of the customers were scantily dressed.

"What have we walked into?" Lucy murmured, spinning her stool toward Justin.

She made the mistake of leaning close enough so they wouldn't be overheard. Immediately, his heat drove into her, making her want to get even closer.

Justin dipped his head so his breath laved her cheek, and longing washed over her.

"Looks like a professional meet-and-greet," he murmured in her ear. "Or you could simply call this a sex club."

"No wonder the cover charge was so high!"

Indeed, the customers in the club appeared to be interested in one thing, and it wasn't the music. Everyone seemed to be coming on to someone—or several someones—in every imaginable combination. Dotted around the club were alcoves with velvet-upholstered booths and curtains that could be pulled for privacy. Some of the occupants should already have pulled them, Lucy thought, getting a load of the action.

"Do they rent rooms upstairs, as well?" she asked, only half-joking.

"Why?" Justin arched an eyebrow. "Want to try one out? We can ask Zeke here."

"Ask Zeke what?" The bartender set a beer and a glass of wine in front of them. "That'll be twenty."

When she got a closer look at Zeke, Lucy realized he was wearing eyeliner and eyeshadow that had been artfully smudged to give him that smoky-eyed look.

Justin gave him a twenty and another five for a tip, but he didn't put away his wallet. "Actually, we do have a couple of questions for you."

"Shoot."

"About a woman who was here three or four weeks ago."

"I'm not sure my memory is all that good."

"Here's some encouragement." Justin slipped him a fifty, which Zeke quickly pocketed.

"I'll see what I can do," he promised.

"Her name's Sophie Delacorte. She reads tarot at Jackson Square."

"Sophie, yeah, sure I know her. She's a regular, tries picking up new clients who want their own psychic. Haven't seen her recently, though."

Not surprising, considering Sophie was dead, but Lucy wouldn't volunteer that info. Nor Justin, either.

"On the night in question, she was with a woman," Justin said. "A tall blonde named Erica Vaughn."

"Doesn't ring a bell."

"Think back hard." He slipped the bartender another fifty for his effort.

"Maybe you'll remember the ring she wore," Lucy said. Zeke looked like the type who would appreciate an eye-popping piece of jewelry—he wore enough gold himself. "*Big* ring, middle finger. topaz and gold inlaid with rubies and emeralds."

"Oh, yeah, I remember that ring, all right. And the woman," he added.

"What is it you remember exactly about Erica Vaughn?" Justin asked.

"Only that she was looking for someone."

"Her sister?" Lucy asked.

"Could be."

"In this club? Her sister's only eighteen—"

"Whoa! We check identification carefully. We can't afford to let underage kids with fake IDs in here. She wasn't here, so don't get your shorts in a twist."

"But Erica did meet Sophie here, right?" Lucy asked. Maybe she thought Sophie could give her answers through the tarot cards.

"No, the blonde came into the club *with* Sophie. They already knew each other."

"Did you get any feel for the type of relationship they had?" Lucy asked. "I mean, was it personal…or something else?"

"Now that I wouldn't know. Do you mean did they act like lovers?" Zeke shrugged. "They had this private thing going on between them, but I wouldn't presume to define it."

She was wondering if another fifty would make a difference when Justin asked, "Did they come in together often?"

"Only that once. Well, that I know of, that is. I do have days off. Listen, I got to get back to work before I get my butt fired."

"Here's my card," Justin said, slipping one across the bar to Zeke. "If you think of anything else, call me."

Zeke shoved the card in his pocket, saying, "You bet," before greeting a customer who'd just taken a stool at the other end of the bar.

Justin took a swallow of beer and said, "Let's get out of here."

Nodding, Lucy finished her glass of wine, then slipped off the stool.

JUSTIN REALIZED they were going to have to make their way back across the crowded dance floor—there were now so many people on the sidelines ogling the dancers that they had no choice. Thinking to protect her from being clunked by one of the gyrating bodies, he slipped an arm around Lucy's waist and pulled her into him. She felt so good, so right pressed up against him, that he never wanted to let her go.

As they inched across the dance floor, the music pulsed at him—a jazz number with a woman singer doing vocalizations that sounded like she was in the middle of having sex.

Glancing down at Lucy, he wanted to hear those sounds coming from her sweet lips. Just not yet. Not until the case was resolved. Until the murderer was behind bars. He'd let his guard down once before and had let a client be killed.

But when a couple knocked into Lucy, sending her flying against him, he couldn't hang on to his resolve.

"One dance?" he asked.

One dance would give him some kind of satisfaction without hurting anything. Without hurting her.

"One dance," she agreed, slipping her arms up around his neck.

Justin groaned as her body stretched along his, teasing every inch of his quickening flesh. Not that this was a new sensation. He'd been hot for her ever since the night in the bayou, when he'd pulled her out of sight of those thugs.

Around them, strangers were making sexual liaisons. They kissed. They touched. They didn't try to hide their desire for one another.

But he had to, and he knew it. For Lucy's sake.

Not that Lucy seemed to mind being in his arms. Her cat stretches against him, the sexy little sounds she made that were almost lost against the orgasmic music, the tips of her nails cutting into the back of his neck—all told him she was as aroused as he. As ready for anything, maybe even a room upstairs, assuming they really were rentable.

Getting a grip, Justin danced her toward the front of the sex club, toward the door that would take them out of this hedonist's den. Lucy looked up, her features filled with a hunger they shared.

Her body slid upward…her lips seduced his mouth to open…her tongue darted inside.

The first thrust of her pointy little tongue almost got him off, right there, without any preliminaries.

God, he wanted her!

The jazz piece was winding to a crescendo, and the vocalization was, as well. The singer's mouth was pressed to the mike as her mating sounds rose to a fever pitch. When she moaned as if coming—the music abruptly ending—so came the room. It sounded as if they were part of the biggest orgy ever, with the most simultaneous orgasms.

Some couples and other pairings held each other and remained on the dance floor, some fled to their alcoves and drew the privacy curtains, a few found a discreet door—the one that led upstairs?—while others rushed to the exit, no doubt determined to find some secluded spot away from the club where they could orgasm for real.

If they hadn't already.

Lucy almost looked as if she had. Though the light in the club was dim, she seemed to have color in her cheeks and her eyes were sexy-sleepy.

Justin couldn't stand it. He was going to have her. And then he wouldn't let her out of his sight. She would have his full protection. Nothing would happen to her, he promised himself.

But as they approached the door, stuck in the crush of bodies he heard a familiar complaint just ahead.

"They stepped all over my shoes. And someone spilled a drink on one of 'em. Just look at 'em! You know these are Italian—"

"Honey, get me back to my place, and I'll lick your shoes clean myself. Naked."

The man groaned. "Baby, you gotta deal. Let's get outta here!"

Lucy grabbed onto Justin's arm and when he looked down her expression had nothing to do with the pseudo-sex they'd had on the dance floor. She'd heard the exchange, too. The thug with the shoe fetish who'd tried to kill her was in the crowd now exploding out the exit door.

"Let's follow him," Lucy said, and Justin didn't disagree.

This might be the break they needed.

LUCY FELT LIKE she was in the middle of a detective movie. A film noir, dark and gritty. This was New Orleans at its most decadent—sex clubs and women willing to lick men's shoes. Now here they were tail-ing a bad guy in hopes that he would lead them to someone even worse.

Like Sophie's murderer…

The horrible thing was that she was still subtly turned on. Lucy was mortified that she'd had so little control of herself on the dance floor. Even knowing she couldn't carry through with the promise, she'd engaged in hot and heavy contact at that club. And she had started it. Guys had a name for girls who made promises they didn't fulfill.

Prick tease…

At least she wasn't vibrating with the need to orgasm as she had been earlier, but her skin seemed to be alive enough to split if Justin touched her just right.

Or maybe it was simply the night.

They were driving with the windows half-open and the lingering heat and increasing humidity made her skin dewy. It was the kind of night that reminded her of sex—hot and sweaty, a natural musk permeating the air.

Good thing they were in a car, and there was no possibility of anything more happening between them, Lucy thought, the responsibility of Justin's safety pressing down on her as brutally as the night itself.

She had to concentrate on something other than sex, Lucy told herself.

"What if he's armed?" she asked.

"I don't intend to get close enough to find out."

"Good intentions often go astray," she said, realizing Mr. Shoe Fetish was headed for the bridge that would take them across the Mississippi.

"I'm not unarmed," Justin stated.

She hadn't felt a gun on him—and they'd been so damn close on the dance floor that she was certain she would have known if he were carrying. "What do you mean?"

"Glove compartment."

Heart thumping, she opened the glove compartment and got a look at the weapon tucked in with the vehicle's manual.

"Is it loaded?"

"Would there be a point to having an unloaded gun?"

Lucy slammed the glove compartment door so she wouldn't have to look at it, saying, "I hate guns!"

"So do I. Luckily, I've never had to use one."

"You mean you've never shot it or that you've never even pointed it at someone."

"Never pointed it."

"Then why have it?"

"I'm a private investigator. I never know when I may need it."

"Let's hope not anytime soon."

She settled back and tried to calm her nerves as they crossed the river. They were headed for the Algiers neighborhood where, she guessed, the woman or Mr. Shoe Fetish lived.

"So why do you think Erica Vaughn was hooked up with Sophie Delacorte?" she asked.

"To find her sister Theresa, I'm sure."

"You don't think she was counting on you to do it?"

"I think she wasn't above taking whatever help she could get. I wasn't getting anywhere. No matter what our bartender Zeke said, fake IDs work all too well. Maybe Sophie spotted Theresa in the club."

"But how did they know each other? Erica and Sophie came in together that night. And apparently, they weren't from the same social circle."

"No they weren't. But a lot of people in New Orleans believe in tarot cards or palmistry or voodoo. Maybe Erica did, as well. Maybe she was one of Sophie's private clients."

"And Sophie might have seen something in the cards that led her to the sex club. That would make sense."

Lucy bought the speculation. But then, why wouldn't she with her history? Most psychics were fakes, sure, but who was to say Sophie Delacorte didn't have the gift. As things stood, they would likely never know for sure.

They'd left the bridge and were driving through Algiers Point, a neighborhood of old Creole cottages and shotgun houses, as different from the French Quarter's two-story buildings with iron-lace edged balconies as one could get. The neighborhood was being improved, and renovation money had been sunk into this street.

Ahead, the car pulled to the curb. Justin slowed and Lucy could see the occupants getting out of the other car. The thug had wrapped his arms around the woman and, to Lucy's disgust, kissed and felt her up right there under a streetlight.

"Where are you going?" she asked when Justin drove past them.

"Ahead a bit. Unless you want me to stop right here and shine a light on them."

"No, of course not."

Lucy watched first through her side-view mirror, then less subtly through the rear window, as the couple broke the embrace and rushed to the door of a Creole cottage. The front porch light was on, and after the woman unlocked the door, the couple took the opportunity to make something of a display of themselves.

Lucy couldn't stop herself from watching them.

It was like a car wreck—you didn't want to look, but you simply couldn't turn away.

Justin pulled over to the curb and cut the lights, waiting only long enough for the thug to follow his "date" inside before bringing the car to life once more. He did a U-turn in the middle of the block, then came back and parked across the street and a short ways down from Mr. Shoe Fetish's car.

"So what's the plan?"

He pulled a notebook from an inner pocket. "First, I'm going to get his license and see if I can't get it checked out, then we wait until he comes out and we follow him. Hopefully he'll lead us to the man you saw kill Sophie Delacorte. If he doesn't, he'll at least lead us to his own place and either I'll stake him out or I'll find someone to do it for me."

"Who would know being a P.I. could be so boring?"

"You're bored with me?"

"I didn't say that. It's the thought of sitting in the car waiting hour after hour that sounds boring." She would keep the interesting activities they could engage in to pass the time to herself.

"There are downsides to every job."

"What's the upside?"

"Reuniting family. Finding someone who just inherited a small fortune. Helping to put someone guilty of insurance fraud where he belongs."

Another reason to like Justin Guidry too much for his own good. She said, "The people connection."

"You got it."

"Too bad you couldn't reunite Erica and Theresa," Lucy said, thinking of the two women who had been murdered. Or was it three? "Do you think Theresa Vaughn is still alive?"

"It's hard to say. I was following her trail and then it was like she fell off the edge of the earth."

"I wonder if Erica and Sophie found her...or found out what happened to her."

"Their discovery of proof that Theresa was murdered could be the reason both women were killed," Justin admitted. "Dead women can't talk."

A fact that made Lucy remind herself of why she and Justin were working on this together. Erica and Sophie had been killed by the same man, and fate had somehow thrown her at Justin to see that these women didn't simply become statistics in the NOPD cold case files.

She decided to concentrate on that before she went to sleep for the night and maybe that would help come up with some answers.

11

His tongue slid along the soft flesh, opening it to his rhythmic stroking. She tangled her fingers in his dark hair and opened herself wider, allowing him deeper access.

He tested her with a finger, never stopping the titillation of his tongue.

His fingers were inside her now. One...two... No more, she couldn't take more. But she wanted more. She would take all of him if she could.

She spread wider...arched higher...trying to hold on.

Lucy orgasmed awake and then experienced a moment's confusion.

Light made her sensitive eyes squinch.

It was morning...

Rather than being liquid as usually happened after she came, she was stiff and sore and leaning sideways. And she felt trapped by a heavy weight. Blinking, she realized sunlight was becoming through the windshield of a car. Justin's car. And that was Justin's weight against her.

He groaned and wriggled around as if starting to awaken also. His mouth was practically at her breast, and even through her clothing, her nipple reacted to the damp warmth of his breath. The sensitive flesh tightened and pushed toward him as if wanting to be suckled.

Damn her dreams!

Trying not to panic, not wanting him to get the wrong idea, Lucy closed her eyes, regulated her breathing and pretended to be asleep.

"Mmm, Lucille…oh, hell!"

With that, Justin apparently awakened and instantly moved away from her. Regretting the loss of his body pressed up against hers only for a moment, Lucy sighed in her supposed "sleep" and blinked her eyes and yawned.

"Mmm, morning," she said in a hoarse whisper. "How did we manage to fall asleep?"

"I guess all that excitement last night did us in," he said drily.

"Coffee," she croaked almost simultaneously with his explosive curse. "What?"

She sat straighter and looking around, expecting to see some baseball-wielding maniac coming at their windshield. Any potential threat eluded her.

"The guy's car," Justin said. "It's gone! He got away while we were asleep."

"You mean we spent the whole night cramped up in this car for nothing?"

"Afraid so."

Back to square one. Lucy moaned. "Great. Just great. Now what?"

"Now we get some coffee."

Justin started the engine, and pulled even with the house they'd been staking out. He made a note in his book—the address, Lucy saw—before heading out.

A few minutes later, they found a nearby place that had enough cars lined up outside to convince them the food must be decent. Justin parked, and they both tumbled out of the car groaning and trying to ease stiff muscles.

The restaurant was small, noisy and packed. Luckily, a couple was just getting up to leave as they entered.

Along with cups of chicory-laced brew, they ate a breakfast that was filling, tasty and cheap. And while Lucy wolfed down her food, she remembered her latest dream and thought about her inability to keep her mind where it belonged. And about Emile's suggestion that she learn to use her gift to her best advantage.

Right now, you're a receiver...learn to be more...

If she tried, could she control her dreams? But how to accomplish that? Wondering if Gran would be able to help her there, Lucy figured there was only one way to find out.

"I have some things to take care of sometime today," Lucy announced as she pushed her mostly empty plate away. She'd eaten so much she felt near to bursting. "Checking in with Dana..." *Paying Gran a visit.*

"This morning is as good a time as any," Justin said. "I have some calls to make. For one, I'm going to try to run down those plates. And two, I'm going to get someone to house-sit in case our shoe-loving thug pays a return visit to his lady."

"Good. So where do we meet up later?" she asked.

"Back at my place after lunch? Hopefully by then I'll have something. At least a plan of action."

"Sounds good."

Very good. Enough time for her to have a heart-to-heart with Gran and put some distance between herself and the man who was turning her world upside down.

AFTER HER BELOVED husband Jake had died of an unexpected heart attack twenty-odd years before, Gran—known to the world as Emma Louise Ryan—had given up ownership of their Greek Revival mansion with its Corinthian columns, double-galleried balcony and twin parlors that opened into a ballroom, to her only son Jack. Her only stipulation had been that she would be allowed to live for the rest of her life in the converted carriage house in the rear.

Though Gran had seemingly retired from the Garden District social circuit, Lucy knew the invitations had never stopped arriving. Everyone had doted on dear, if eccentric, Emma Louise. And, of course, Gran had eventually risen above her grief to renew old friendships. While growing up, Lucy had spent much of her free time there with Gran, the one person in the world who had always understood her.

Opening the black wrought iron gate with its familiar vine and rose design, nature's perfume—the scent of the magnolia trees and flowering plants—welcomed her. The garden surrounding the carriage house had always been and was still Gran's domain, and Lucy had often helped her tend to the beds.

As if she knew Lucy was coming, Gran was waiting in the doorway for her. She hadn't changed much since Lucy was a child. She merely had a bit more gray in her fading reddish-brown hair, and a few more wrinkles at the corners of her gray eyes so like Lucy's own. But now in her early eighties, Gran was still youthfully trim. As always, she was elegantly dressed in pale rose trousers and a cream silk blouse as if she were ready to go to one of her Garden District Preservation Committee meetings.

Once inside, Lucy threw her arms around Gran's shoulders and kissed her on both cheeks. "It's so good to see you."

Squeezing and kissing Lucy in return, Gran said, "Some lovely young people make it a point to visit their grandmothers on a more regular basis."

"I see you as often as I do my parents," Lucy protested.

"It's not nearly enough."

An argument Lucy wasn't bound to win. Sighing, she said, "Yes, ma'am, I get the message."

Gran's bowed lips pulled into a foxy smile. "Good. Then we'll set a date for a proper visit before you leave." She fanned herself. "It's passing hot this morning. Can I get you some lemonade or iced tea?"

"Tea, please."

Lucy followed Gran into her kitchen, old-fashioned but still charming with melon-colored walls and a collection of fanciful teapots lining long shelves below the mahogany wall cabinets. Her grandmother usually only made herself breakfast and lunch and went up to the main house for dinner. And why not when Lucy's mother had a part-time cook in addition to the full-time housekeeper?

Parking herself at the kitchen table, watching her grandmother fill two tall glasses with ice cubes, Lucy stalled, wondering how to begin.

"So what's troubling you, child?" Gran prompted her.

"How can you tell?"

"I've been sensing something was wrong with you for a few days now."

That didn't surprise Lucy. Her grandmother's psychic abilities went far beyond her own.

"You sensed something was wrong and you didn't call me to find out what?"

Gran pulled a pitcher of tea from the refrigerator and filled the glasses. "You're not a child anymore. I knew you would come to me to talk about whatever it was when you were ready. When I awoke this morning, I knew today would be the day."

Lucy wondered how much else her grandmother knew. Gran might not be able to read *her* dreams, but she could have warning dreams of her own.

"No, I don't know what's troubling you, Lucy." Gran set a glass on the table before her. "Or I wouldn't have asked."

A chill shot up Lucy's spine. It was as if Gran had heard what she was thinking. She waited until Gran took the seat opposite her. Then she searched for a way to begin that was far more casual than she was feeling. She didn't want to alarm her grandmother.

"A couple of things are bothering me, actually."

She gave Gran an abbreviated summary of the dreams that had been plaguing her, talking about seeing "romantic moments" with Justin rather than "erotic encounters."

Gran's eyebrows raised. "And this would be a problem…why?"

"Gra-a-an! I have more important things on my mind than…well, romance." She'd almost said sex.

"Like what?"

No way she was going to tell Gran about the murder, so she danced around it. "Something that's important to me. Something I want to, well, let's call it research. I want to dream about *that*, instead of…romance."

"Maybe if you told me more about whatever *that* was?"

Gran was frowning now, and Lucy feared she was getting some kind of reading off her, and that with a little effort, she would know everything.

"Look, the reason I came to see you was to find out if it was possible to push my dreams in a particular direction, to use them as a tool to get this information I need to have. Have you ever been able to pull that off?"

"At times," Gran said before switching subjects. "So you *don't* want to dream about this young man of yours?"

"No! And Justin isn't mine."

"Then why do you have that nice color in your face when you think about this Justin?" Gran's eyes widened. "Oh, *those* kind of dreams."

Rather than appearing horrified, she seemed amused, Lucy realized, wanting to sink right through the floor. And from somewhere came a vague memory of her earthy grandmother giving her the sex talk that her mother had refused after saying a well-bred lady never discussed such things.

Gran said, "Well, it's about time you got serious with someone."

"Who said I was serious about anyone?"

"Your dreams, child, your dreams. When you can't control them…he's got to be the one."

"No, he can't be."

"I don't believe you have anything to say about it. Some things are simply destined."

If that were true, Justin would be shot because of her. "I *must* have something to say about it," Lucy muttered. "I can't just let that happen."

"Lucy, what's going on?"

She looked up to meet her grandmother's worried expression. Great. Just what she hadn't wanted to do was alarm Gram.

"The situation is complicated, Gran. Trust me, and I'll tell you everything when I can, I promise. In the meantime, can't you just help me out here?" Lucy pleaded.

Though she seemed uncertain, Gran nodded. "Of course I trust you. You've always been a good girl, always done what was right."

Relief washed through Lucy. "Thank you. So what do I do to get the dreams I want?"

"Don't wait for them to come to you. Decide where you want your mind to take you."

"I tried that," Lucy said, thinking of the car scenario. "Didn't work."

"You have to *make* the dreams come."

"How is that even possible?"

"Anything is possible," Gran insisted. "You've allowed your gift to develop at its own pace, but you've never tried to master it before, so the fact that you didn't succeed the first time isn't surprising. Liken the process to self-hypnosis. Before you go to sleep, concentrate on the question. Lose yourself in it to the exclusion of everything else. If your will is strong enough—and knowing you, I believe it can be—your dream will give you the answer."

"You make it sound so easy."

"No one said it would be easy. Knowing is never easy." Gran got a faraway look in her eyes and murmured, "Sometimes I think knowing what's going to happen to someone you care about is the heaviest burden in the world, because no matter how hard you try, you simply can't change fate."

Lucy nearly choked on her tea. Certain that Gran meant Justin's getting shot because of her, she asked, "How in the world did you know?"

Gran started. "Oh, dear." Then took a deep breath. "Well, I guess there's no harm in telling you now. At sixty, your grandfather was a virile, healthy man, and when I had a vision of him having that heart attack watching the bonfires on the Mississippi. I made him go to the doctor and tried to change everything I could, from his diet to his exercise program to where we spent Christmas that year. But it didn't matter. There were no bonfires at our resort in South Carolina, but I saw my Jake die anyway. I simply couldn't do anything to stop it from happening."

Horrified, Lucy stared at her grandmother, whose eyes shone with unshed tears. "Gran, you never told me."

"I never told anyone. Not before. Not after. First I didn't want it to be true. Then I couldn't forgive myself."

"It wasn't your fault."

"No," Gran said.

But Lucy knew Gran still felt responsible.

Like *she* would feel responsible if she couldn't keep Justin from dying because of her.

And according to Gran, she couldn't do anything to stop it from happening.

Too much information! Certainly far more than she'd come to get. A little freaked, Lucy tried to hide what she was feeling with little success if the subtle shift in her grandmother's expression were any indication.

"Lucy, what is it?"

"You just got me a little emotional here, is all." That was true enough. "Now when did you want to have that grandmother-granddaughter hot night on the town?"

Gran's serious expression softened a bit. "I know

you're joking, but you might be surprised at some of the things I did when I was a young woman.''

"Maybe you shouldn't tell me." Lucy rolled her eyes. "Better I keep my illusions.''

"THIS IS IT,'' Justin said when they arrived at the Vaughn home on Esplanade late that afternoon.

He tried to take Lucy's arm as they ascended the steps, but she avoided him and rushed ahead, saying, "I still think you should have called first.''

"Too easy for them to say no.''

"Right, this is better,'' she said as he caught up to her on the porch. "You'll shock them into letting us in.''

Now why was it that he'd missed Lucy Ryan practically the whole time they'd been separated? In the few hours he'd been alone, all he'd been able to think about was seeing her again. And now their being together should seem like the most natural thing in the world.

If only Lucy was acting like herself...

Ever since they'd hooked up at his place, she'd been by turns distant and sharp with him. Clearly her excursion that morning had put her in such a rotten mood, but he didn't want to push her to talk about it until she was ready to.

The door opened and a rumpled-looking man with tufts of dark hair poking out from a long, thin face, frowned at them. "Can I help you?''

"Are you Mr. Vaughn?'' Lucy asked.

"Yes.''

"It's about Erica," Justin said. "We're investigating her murder."

"More new detectives? How is the NOPD ever supposed to solve anything if they keep switching you people around on cases?"

"We're not from the department," Lucy admitted.

"Then what the hell are you doing wasting my time? Reporters?" he spat, backing in and apparently meaning to slam the door on them.

"Wait!" Justin said. "Erica may have mentioned me—Justin Guidry." He was relieved when Samuel Vaughn hesitated with his hand on the door. "She hired me to find Theresa."

The sour expression lifted to one more hopeful, as Vaughn asked, "You found my baby?"

Justin wished the man hadn't jumped to the wrong conclusion. Gut knotted, he said, "I'm afraid not. But I'm convinced Erica's murder is connected to Theresa's disappearance and to the murder of another woman a few nights ago."

"No, that can't be right." Vaughn ran a hand through his hair, smoothing it so it lay flat on his head. "Erica was mugged for her money on the Moonwalk and she must have fought the guy. Then he knifed her."

"Something else has recently happened to convince me her death was premeditated murder." Justin glanced at Lucy, who'd glanced away, as if she were thinking of something else. "Another woman, Sophie Delacorte was walking alone late at night, and she was also knifed to death, this time in a courtyard in the

French Quarter. The thing is, Sophie and Erica knew each other.''

He watched a range of emotions wash over the bereaved father's face before he nodded and said, ''Come in,'' then stood back and let them pass.

The beauty of the parlor, decorated with antique pieces was camouflaged by stacks of newspapers and dishes and cups on every surface. Bed pillows and a sheet were strewn on the couch, as if Vaughn had just been sleeping there. Apparently the place had gone to hell over the past several weeks. Justin didn't blame the Vaughns. As the parents of one daughter dead, the other missing, they *were* in hell.

Vaughn asked, ''Does Homicide know about this connection between the two women?''

''Not yet, but they will. Detective Mike Hebert is a friend of mine and I'll be getting him up to speed tonight.''

''Hebert. He seems like a straight-shooter.''

''And a good detective.''

''So why not leave it to him?''

''I feel like I owe it to Erica to help if I can.''

Vaughn turned his gaze to Lucy, who hadn't spoken a word since they'd come inside. Justin was beginning to worry about her. Her being so quiet wasn't like her, and now she'd turned ashen as she stared down at the stack of newspapers. Justin saw she was looking at a story covering Erica Vaughn's murder.

''You, Ms....'' Vaughn said. ''What about you?''

''Lucy Ryan,'' she said, suddenly coming to life, her voice trembling. ''I—I wanted to find Sophie's

murderer. So Justin and I...we kind of hooked up."
She looked around at the mess. "Is Mrs. Vaughn
home?"

"Janet isn't a well woman. Losing both our daughters was too much for her. She's being taken care of
away from the city. I'm not sure she'll ever want to
come back."

"I'm so sorry."

Vaughn bobbed his head. "Maybe if the murderer
was caught...and we found out what happened to our
Theresa, she would... So, tell me how I can help
you."

Justin said, "Let us see Theresa's room, go through
her things."

He hadn't gotten around to that before. He'd wanted
to, but Erica had thought it would be easier on her
delicately nerved mother if she, rather than a stranger,
searched her sister's room. Now Justin regretted letting
her have her way. Maybe if he hadn't, Erica would
still be alive.

"Follow me."

Sam Vaughn led the way up the stairs and down
the hall to a room overlooking the garden. While a
little frilly, Justin got the idea those touches were left
over from Theresa's younger years. The girl had serious electronic equipment on a shelf and a laptop on
her desk.

A phone in the other room rang and Vaughn said,
"I'm expecting a business call. I'm sorry but I have
to take it. I can't afford to lose my job. I may be a
while."

"Take your time."

The man rushed out, leaving Justin alone with Lucy. She stood in the middle of the room and looked around as if she were in a daze.

Justin moved in closer, asking, "Are you all right?"

"What?" She met his gaze. "All right…yeah, sure."

"You seem a little out of it." Or nervous. Around him? Why? "I thought maybe you were coming down with something," he said in an effort to get her to open up.

"Maybe a little tired. And distracted. As soon as we're through here, I need to get over to Bal Masque. So let's get on with it," she said, walking over to the nightstand and checking the drawers.

Whatever was bothering her, Lucy obviously wasn't going to talk about it. Maybe it had to do with her shop. Or a disagreement with her business partner. Or not. It could simply be something personal.

Uneasy without knowing why, Justin took his cue from her and sat himself down in front of the laptop. The police hadn't touched it as far as he knew—they hadn't had much interest in the case. Though Erica had gone through the computer files with no success, Justin knew she could have missed something and so searched for documents that might mention Theresa's married lover.

In between, he kept track of Lucy's movements around the room as she silently searched every drawer from the nightstand to the chest of drawers to the dresser.

She wasn't acting like herself, no doubt about it. Justin wanted to take her in his arms and get her to tell him what was wrong. Not that he could do so here or now. Not that he even knew her well enough to have her trust him with her problems, whether professional or personal.

And yet...

Justin felt as if he'd known Lucy far longer than their actual acquaintance. Spending so much time together must account for that, because he'd become familiar with all her nuances. And this change in her disturbed him. He cared for Lucy on a deeper level than made him comfortable. He tried to tell himself that such a close connection would inevitably happen with any two people thrown together in like circumstances, but he couldn't quite swallow the rationalization.

And so he put the puzzle to the back of his mind and concentrated on the case, beginning by going through Theresa's e-mails. Clearly she didn't kiss and tell. Or she'd done a good job clearing her hard drive of anything incriminating. And it would take a computer geek to get into it to find any e-mails that had been erased. Theoretically, anything deleted was still on the hard drive, waiting like a ghost to be resurrected.

Justin spun around in the chair to find Lucy perched on the edge of Theresa's bed, a book in hand. Her expression was intent as she read.

"Find something interesting?" he asked.

"Not so far, but I'm hoping." Lucy held up what she was reading. "Theresa's diary."

Justin rose and crossed to the bed. "Erica said she didn't keep one."

"Check out the cover. A fake. It looks like a textbook."

"How did you know to look inside?"

"I have a sister, too."

Justin sat next to Lucy. A mistake. The bedsprings squeaked and the mattress sagged, bringing them close enough that he inhaled her scent. He tried holding himself rigidly enough away from her that he wouldn't be turned on, but it was no use. He was fighting a losing battle.

"So, any revelations?" he asked.

"Nothing tangible. References to her lover and descriptions of the things they did together."

Nothing he needed to read, Justin thought, knowing doing so would make being near Lucy unbearable. "But no names. Just a single initial—C."

"That's a big help."

"Wait…" Then she looked up, her expression triumphant. "He's a politician!"

"Well, that narrows it down."

"Listen to this," she said impatiently. "'C is so handsome and charming that the reelection is a done deal. Then he can leave his wife and devote himself to me like he promised.'" Her eyes sparkled with excitement as she said, "That does narrow it down! A handsome and charming politician whose name begins with *C* running for reelection. How many men can fit that description?''

Justin couldn't believe it. The lifting of her sour mood was turning him on. Though he was glad, he was also thankful that he had reason to get off the bed and put a safe distance between them.

''Why don't we find out?''

Even as he asked it, Sam Vaughn came back into the room. ''You folks find anything?''

Lucy quickly reiterated what she'd just told Justin, asking, ''Do you mind if I take the diary with me, Mr. Vaughn? Maybe if I keep reading, I'll find something more specific about this mysterious politician.''

''Politicians!'' Vaughn cursed under his breath. ''Take it, but promise me you'll give this information to the detective. The police haven't really done anything for us up to this point. Maybe if you tell them what you told me—''

''We will,'' Lucy quickly promised.

Justin planned on it, though he didn't know if it would set any wheels in motion or not. He hoped the Erica and Sophie connection might do the trick.

''We should take the laptop, as well,'' Justin said. ''I couldn't find anything in Theresa's e-mails, but I would bet the man she was seeing sent her e-mails and even if she deleted them, an expert could probably pull them back up.''

''Take what you need,'' Vaughn said.

''I want to thank you for your cooperation, and I promise that we'll share whatever we learn with Detective Hebert.''

"It's you who should get the thanks. Both of you."
Vaughn's eyes filled with tears. "I don't know which
is worse—having one of my daughters dead or not
knowing the whereabouts of the other."

They left with the laptop and diary.

"I think I'll head straight for Bal Masque," Lucy
said, beating him down the steps. "So maybe you
ought to take that stuff to your place and I'll catch up
with you later."

"Whoa, wait a minute. I'll give you a ride."

She turned to face him, but kept walking backwards.
"I need the exercise. It'll feel good to stretch my
legs."

Reluctant to let her out of his sight, Justin had to
force him to say, "Fine. Later, then."

Justin got in the car, and sat there feeling oddly
bereft as he watched Lucy head down the street. Only
when she turned the corner and disappeared from sight
did he start the car and head for his place.

He had to get over this…well, whatever it was he
was feeling for Lucy Ryan. She'd had a spring in her
step quite different from the way she'd been earlier.
He couldn't help but think it was because of him—
she couldn't get away from him quickly enough.

12

WHEN LUCY arrived at Bal Masque the shop was busy, so she ignored her partner's surprised expression and pitched in and took care of customers.

But when the shop cleared out, Dana immediately jumped on her. "Okay, it's just you and me here. How long do I have to stay at my sister's?"

"Hopefully not much longer."

"Oh, yeah, that's real specific. What's going on with you? Spill!"

Lucy sighed. "Well, it all started when I dreamed about a woman being murdered. I tried to stop it from happening, but I was too late. And the murderer knows I saw."

She gave Dana an abbreviated version of her predicament, from being chased by the thugs straight into Justin's arms to Gran's insistence that she couldn't change anything that she'd seen.

"So according to your grandmother," Dana said thoughtfully, "Justin is the man for you."

Amazed that her friend had chosen that specific piece of information to elaborate on rather than the deaths, Lucy said, "Yeah, until he gets shot and dies."

"Did you *see* him die?"

"Well, no." That didn't mean he wouldn't, Lucy thought morosely. In the shooting dream, Justin had been focused on *her*, and she hadn't seen a weapon. He wouldn't stand a chance, no more than either Erica or Sophie. "But Sophie Delacorte did, remember. I was hoping that if we could only figure out the identity of the murderer, we could have him arrested and Justin would be safe."

"Maybe he will be."

"Not according to what Gran said."

"So what are you going to do?"

"I don't have a clue. I was hoping that talking to someone practical like you would help."

"If I was truly practical, I wouldn't believe in psychic dreams," Dana said, brushing a strand of blond hair out of her eyes. "Then, again, I've been around you for too long not to." She frowned, thought for a moment, then said, "The dreams give you an edge. Time to deal with things, to figure out how to handle the situations before they come up."

That was the Dana she knew, the one who could help her figure out this mess. "Maybe I could do something positive if I could control the dreams."

"Then you need to try. Either do that or get out of the city until the murder is solved. I know you. If you stay, you won't leave it alone."

"How can I?"

"You're not responsible, Lucy."

"But I feel like I am."

"Maybe the dreams aren't telling you to interfere but to get out while the going is good. Get out of the way and let the professionals handle it.'' When Lucy didn't respond, Dana said, ''Uh-huh.''

''You know I can't.''

''But you *can* be careful. And you can allow yourself to believe in the good dreams, too.''

''Justin?''

''Go for a chance at happiness. Sleep with the man, for heaven's sake.''

Heat shot through Lucy. That's exactly what she wanted. ''But if I do, then the rest will come true.''

''According to your grandmother, it will *all* come true no matter what you do or don't do.''

Her friend had a point, but still…

''Do you like the man?'' Dana asked. ''Do you want to sleep with him?''

''Yes, but—''

''Do you think he wants to sleep with you?''

Lucy felt her face reddening and began straightening a table of inexpensive sparkly masks. ''Maybe…I don't know.''

''He wouldn't have pulled that love potion ploy yesterday, if having sex with you wasn't on his mind. Do you see yourself making it with a Justin Guidry?''

''In dreams, yes.''

''Is that really the problem then?'' Dana asked. ''You don't see yourself with him in real life. You're not sure that a man like Justin could really be attracted to boring old you, so you won't act on your own instincts.''

''That's ridiculous. None of that even entered my head.''

"Well, maybe you should consider it. Your evaluation of yourself as a non-guy-magnet has been in your subconscious like forever. Well, as long as I've known you, anyway, which is almost all our lives. You've had this buddy thing going on long enough, don't you think?"

"That's what guys seem to want from me, so what's wrong with it?" Lucy asked. Not that she'd been virginal before Justin, but she'd gone into sexual relationships with men in a realistic manner. "Everyone can use friends."

Dana shook her head. "Lucy, Lucy, Lucy. It's time you stopped second-guessing yourself. You're talented and smart and attractive. What's not to want?"

Even hearing her best friend describe her like that made Lucy shift uncomfortably. "So *you* think I've put up some kind of a barrier because I don't think I'm worthy."

Which was the biggest crock, Lucy thought. She had her share of confidence.

"Unconsciously, you could be doing that, sure. Unless it's *something else* keeping you from claiming the passion in your life that you deserve."

"I *have* passion."

"In your artwork, yes. But when was the last time you went on a really hot date. Pre-Justin, that is."

"Justin and I aren't dating—"

They didn't have time to continue the discussion. To Lucy's relief, customers flooded the shop and suddenly break time was over.

But even as she waited on a woman who was considering buying one of the more expensive masks, Lucy mulled over Dana's examination of her life. Was her friend correct? Had she used excuses to unconsciously exclude passion from her life? Why in the world would she purposely do that? She was as red-blooded and healthy as any woman her age ought to be.

It came to her suddenly. The dreams. *They* made her different. And it was difficult for her to relate to someone who might scoff at her. A close relationship demanded that she be honest about it. But as she'd been warned by her parents and sister for years, not many people understood or accepted psychic visions.

Yet, a self-described disbeliever, Justin had.

The train of thought jolted Lucy. That she'd been holding herself back from getting too involved with a man was a distinct possibility. But she didn't manipulate her dreams. She hadn't even thought she could or wanted to try until Emile Poree had suggested it was possible, that she might be able to use her gift to find Sophie's murderer.

But what if she *had* manipulated some of her dreams subconsciously? What if she had given herself a reason *not* to get involved with Justin Guidry. What if her subconscious mind had prompted the shooting dream so she would have a reason not to get too deeply involved with him.

Something to consider.

But how would she know for certain?

JUSTIN SPENT the rest of the morning trying not to think about Lucy. Arriving back at his loft, he collected several messages—clients and potential clients—and lined up a number of appointments for the coming week. Next he called a contact who assured him he'd have the name and address that went with the thug's license plate before the end of the day.

Then he sat down at his computer and connected to the Internet to find any candidates up for reelection in November whose first or last name began with the letter *C*.

But as he searched for election information, he wished Lucy was alongside him so he could get her input. As investigators, they made a good team.

What kind of a team would they make as a couple? He kept wondering where Lucy was now, what she was doing, when she would be back. The work wouldn't seem so tedious with her at his side. He checked his watch. He'd been with her just two hours ago, yet the time was passing so slowly that it seemed much longer.

Justin forced the thought from his mind and concentrated on the list of candidates for the November election—federal, state, local. He pulled off anyone with the initial C, either first or last name, then eliminated the women. He was left with a list of thirteen.

Next, he eliminated anyone who was up for election for the first time, which left him with seven potential suspects.

Needing a break, Justin got up and stretched, then put on a pot of fresh coffee. While it was brewing, he wandered over to the windows facing the street. He stood there staring for several minutes before he realized he was looking for a certain russet-haired female.

He had Lucy on the brain...not to mention other parts of his body.

So, back to work.

In the end, two men fit the requirements: councilman-at-large Charles Cahill and Louisiana senator Carlin Montgomery. The other *C*s included one man in his seventies and another who wouldn't be considered handsome by any stretch of the imagination, not even by his own mother. Plus there were a couple of single guys, including one who was running on an openly homosexual agenda.

Justin went straight to his suspects' Web sites. He scanned the material there—not that he got any clues from the professionally written bios.

The phone buzzed, signaling someone was at the intercom downstairs. Pulse quickening, he answered, "Guidry here."

"I'm back," came Lucy's all-too-welcome voice.

"I'll buzz you right up."

He did so, then got up to open the door. Passing a mirror, he stopped to straighten his shirt collar and scrape the hair up from his forehead. Realizing he was being ridiculously self-conscious, he opened the door and then went back to the computer. He didn't want to seem too anxious.

But when Lucy burst through the door, she brought a ray of sunshine into his heart and he couldn't stop from grinning at her. "About time."

"You're not the only one who has a business. So how is it going?"

"Getting there," he said.

Lucy came to stand behind him. When she leaned over to see the computer screen, her scent washed over him, and it was all Justin could do to not reach around and pull her into his lap.

He printed out two photos of each of the suspects, one set which he handed to Lucy. He folded the second set and put it in his pocket.

"Wow, these guys look pretty old to be messing around with someone who's barely legal."

"Montgomery must be in his mid-forties," Justin said. "But Cahill is probably ten years younger."

"Still twice Theresa's age." Lucy made a sound of disgust. "You men are all alike when it comes to women. What do we do next?"

"We call Mike."

"Your thirty-six hours isn't up."

"But now we have suspects," Justin reasoned. "Mike might have some ideas here. He might know something about one of these men that we don't. Besides, he can get an expert to work on retrieving the deleted e-mails on Theresa's laptop. Then it would be all over."

An idea that had mixed appeal for him, all over meaning he might not ever see Lucy again.

"Why wouldn't they have done that before?"

"There wasn't any evidence of foul play. Theresa was merely missing, and as an almost-adult, that's allowed."

"Okay. It's your call," she said.

And Justin made it. The detective agreed to meet them in half an hour on the Moonwalk.

Justin took Theresa's laptop and Lucy the diary before heading for the French Quarter.

LUCY WAS ON EDGE by the time they arrived at the Moonwalk ten minutes ahead of time. Luckily, they found a vacant bench, where they could sit and look out on the Mississippi. Almost like they were on a date.

Only this was no date. This could be it. With the NOPD having all the information, the case could be solved in a matter of days.

And then she could breathe easy once again.

"I'll be glad when this is over," Lucy said.

Suddenly it hit her squarely in the chest how much she would miss Justin. She squeezed the diary, thinking of how Theresa must have felt knowing the man she wanted was unavailable to her. Not that Justin was married, of course.

"This whole mess is a big disruption in your life," he agreed, not sounding at all like he would miss her.

Lucy swallowed hard. "I'll be able to get back to work rather than just stopping in the shop to see how things are going."

"And you'll be able to do your art."

"When I have time."

"You don't make the time?"

"Not often enough."

"You should. Your work is wonderful, *chère*."

His words warmed her. "How would you know?"

"The masks on your living room walls. You did initial them."

"You're very observant."

"That's what makes me a good investigator."

"About that. Why?"

"I thought about going into law enforcement," Justin said, "but wearing a uniform didn't suit me."

"I think you'd look pretty good in a uniform."

Lucy couldn't help herself. She was flirting with him and she knew it. The flare in his eyes told her he knew it, as well. That look was all it took to jump-start her hormones.

"I had other reasons for not joining the force," Justin admitted. "I never took much to taking orders. And I like to work on my own."

"So you're a loner."

"Usually. Comes from having too much family in my life, I suppose."

A statement that Lucy didn't understand. "You can never have too much family. Well, not in my opinion. Plus, I don't see how you can say that considering how close you seem to be to yours."

"Close at a distance suits me fine. I grew up not having a private thought."

"And I grew up having too many of them," she remembered.

"Your family's not close?"

"Certainly not the way yours is. And then there's the matter of my gift. It caused me a lot of confusion and heartache, especially since Gran was the only one I could go to about it.''

Though part of her thought—hoped—that she could tell Justin anything, as well.

He said, ''I'm guessing you haven't told her the latest, right?''

''The latest?''

She felt heat gather in her cheeks as she remembered the dreams and realized Justin was staring at her with hunger in his eyes.

Then he snapped out of it and said, ''The murder.''

''No, of course not,'' she said in an embarrassed rush. ''I wouldn't want to upset Gran like that.''

If it meant involving her grandmother in something so awful, she would rather keep it to herself. Actually, this wasn't the first time she'd kept her dreams to herself, which had made for a somewhat lonely childhood and, indeed, a somewhat lonely life.

Justin looked over her shoulder and said, ''There's Mike.''

Lucy turned to see Detective Mike Hebert coming down the walk toward them.

They rose and met him halfway.

''Justin. Ms. Ryan.''

''Lucy,'' she said.

Mike nodded, then turned his attention to Justin. ''Your calling me was certainly a surprise. I was pretty sure I was going to have to track you down to get you to hold to your end of the bargain. So what did the two of you dig up that was so important?''

Justin said, "How about a link between two murder victims and a couple of suspects."

"How's that?"

"The bordello tarot cards you told us about—I'd seen them before," Lucy explained, "at a shop called Taboo."

"I know it. Odette LaFantary's place."

"She told us that a tarot dealer named Sophie bought the deck to use with a special client."

"Sophie," Mike repeated. "So that's the name of the woman in the courtyard?"

"Sophie Delacorte," Justin said. "One of the Jackson Square psychics knows her. He told us about seeing her at a place called Music of the Night. And the bartender at the club saw her with Erica Vaughn."

The detective cursed under his breath. "Together, huh? You're right. They must be connected. Good work." He sounded impressed. "But you said something about suspects?"

Lucy said, "We learned Theresa Vaughn was seeing a married politician up for reelection. And we know his name begins with a *C.*"

"And you learned this how?"

"We went to her home and talked to her father," Justin said. "Then I researched who was up for reelection and narrowed it down."

"Don't keep me guessing," Mike said.

"I'd stake my reputation on the murderer of both women being either councilman-at-large Charles Cahill or Louisiana senator Carlin Montgomery."

The detective gave a low whistle. "High flyers."

"The reason I decided to turn over the information to you as soon as possible. Oh, yeah, and this." Justin produced the laptop. "It belonged to Theresa."

"You found something more direct?"

"Sorry. I expected e-mails at the least, but she was very careful to hit the delete key and empty the trash. I figured you have someone who would know how to retrieve that kind of information."

"Thanks," Mike said, taking the laptop from him. "I'll see what our lab can do."

"If we work together on this," Justin said, "we can catch the bastard."

"Work together? You know that's impossible."

"I didn't mean in the open. Anything you learn, you let me know."

Mike shook his head. "I think it's time you left the investigation to us."

"You had weeks to come up with information," Lucy said, irritated on Justin's behalf. And her own, though of course the detective didn't know her true role in this. She crushed the diary to her chest. "We had thirty-six hours—"

"Sorry," Mike interrupted. "But it's for your own sake. I can't do anything that would put civilians in jeopardy. It wouldn't be safe for you, and it could mean my job. I thank you for the information, but it's time for you to bow out."

"Bow out?" Lucy nearly choked on the words. If only she could turn around and walk away without jeopardizing her life…not to mention abandoning Justin.

"C'mon, Mike, we were upfront with you," Justin reasoned, "the least you could do is return the favor."

"It's you who is returning the favor—I gave you the info on the tarot deck in the first place."

"One piece of information," Justin argued. "We gave you suspects."

"Again, good work and thanks. But I can't involve you further."

Lucy heard the thread of steel in the detective's voice. Though she'd meant to give him Theresa's diary also, she changed her mind. He could have it when she was through with it.

"You do what you have to," she said, "and we'll do what we have to."

"Don't take it on yourself to do anything foolish," the detective warned her. "Unless you don't care about your life. We're dealing with a multiple-murderer here."

But that was the problem. Lucy thought. She did care about her life. And about Sophie's and Erica's and Theresa's. Still, there was no point in arguing the issue. Mike obviously had made up his mind.

And Justin was holding in his anger, she realized. She practically could see it come off him in waves. But he kept it to himself and bade the detective a civil adieu. Mike looked back at them only once as he walked away with Theresa Vaughn's laptop.

"Maybe he's right," Justin said.

"The hell he is. I'm not stopping." She tapped the diary against her palm. "You can do what pleases you."

"It's not a matter of my pleasure. I'm only worried for your safety."

"And how is doing nothing going to keep me safe?"

"Doing nothing as far away from New Orleans as you can get would certainly keep you safe."

"I'm not running away. Not again. What if Theresa Vaughn is still alive?"

"That's highly unlikely, and you know it."

"I don't know anything of the sort. And until I do..."

"So if they found her body today, you would leave town until the murderer is caught?"

Why was he doing this to her now, when they were hot on the murderer's trail?

"When we get back to your place, I'm going to go through that diary line-by-line and see what I can find out. That is, assuming I'm still welcome at your place."

"You'll always be welcome, *chère.*"

Justin's voice was low and gravelly, but Lucy ignored the shivery sensation along her spine. He was simply trying to distract her.

"Then let's get going."

They returned directly to the loft. Justin called a local place to have a couple of dinners delivered, while Lucy began reading the diary, starting with the most recent entries and going backward. Then he sat down at the computer and began researching both politicians, occasionally sharing or printing something he'd found.

To Lucy's satisfaction and dismay, several entries in the diary indicated C. had taken Theresa to a club where "people did things she'd never known anyone would do in public."

The phone buzzed and Lucy half listened as she continued reading. The food delivery guy had arrived with dinner. Justin buzzed the guy up, and she continued to read until the bags of food were on the counter and Justin was taking out dishes and flatware.

"Music of the Night," she told him, after reading another passage. "She only calls it the club, but considering some of her observations, it's clear that she's describing the activities at a sex club. She's only eighteen, but the bastard took her there! Zeke lied."

"Not necessarily. She probably had good fake IDs. However, I have a couple of photos of Theresa that her sister gave me, and we ought to take them to the club tonight, show them around and see what we can find out."

Instinct told Lucy that Zeke knew more than he'd let on. If only they could figure out a way to make him talk.

She tried concentrating on figuring a way to do so as they sat down to eat, but what came to her was that once more, she would be entering a sexually charged atmosphere with a man she wanted more than anything. She already felt herself getting weak-kneed and wondered how long she would be able to resist making love with Justin Guidry and having probably the best sex of her life.

13

IN THE END, Justin decided to take not only the photos of Theresa with them, but the prints of Cahill and Montgomery that he'd gotten off the Internet. He also printed out a story that hadn't meant anything to him when he'd first seen it online.

"According to this," he said, giving Lucy the print-out, "councilman-at-large Charles Cahill is accusing Louisiana senator Carlin Montgomery of taking bribes."

"What?" Appearing as shocked as he felt, she scanned the article. "Our two suspects at odds and in public. Do you think the accusation is true?"

"Good question. It could simply be politics as usual."

"Yeah, but what if it isn't? What if Montgomery is guilty and Theresa somehow found out about it?"

A possibility that he himself had considered. "Surely Mike knew about this, but he chose not to say anything. Maybe that was the reason he cut us off."

"I don't understand. Why would he do that?"

That's what Justin wanted to know. "I don't know what's going on, but the department obviously has

Montgomery under investigation, and Montgomery being who he is and all…well, that might put Mike in a tough spot.''

"So you think he won't use the information?'' Lucy asked, spots of color flaring to her cheeks.

"I think he'll probably use it, but quietly until he's sure of what he has.

"That won't stop us, I hope.''

"Not for a second. Let's get going.''

Justin had wanted to keep focused on the case, but returning to the sex club with Lucy at his side was one hell of a temptation to put his own needs—and hopefully hers—first. Dressed in a little black outfit that showed off her curves and revealed several inches of smooth skin at her waist, Lucy Ryan looked hotter than he'd ever seen her.

Justin couldn't help himself. As they stepped into the club, he slid a hand around that exposed skin. The bandage was gone, though he could still tell the flesh had been nicked by a bullet. That healing flesh quivered under his palm and he heard the sexy little catch in her breath. He stared down into her eyes and nearly lost himself. But the thunderous beat of the music and the growing tension in the crowd drew him back to his surroundings.

Justin swiftly guided Lucy across the dance floor before they could get caught in the midst of sex-fever as they had the last time.

If his raised eyebrows were any indication, Zeke had spotted them as they approached his bar. But the bartender was taking an order and didn't acknowledge them directly. He began making drinks as Justin held the only empty stool for Lucy.

"Do you think he's purposely ignoring us?" she asked, her mouth practically to his ear.

The resulting sensation had Justin fighting for his equilibrium. "He's taking his time. Upping the ante." Justin had no doubts that Zeke would expect big bucks for more information.

Eventually Zeke got around to them and asked, "What can I do for you?"

"The usual."

"Information." Zeke nodded. "What kind?"

Lucy slid a couple of photos of Theresa at him. "When was the last time you saw this woman in here?"

Zeke glanced at the photos and shrugged. "I'm not sure that I have seen her."

Without comment, Justin slipped him the required gratuity.

Though he took it, Zeke said, "Really, I don't know if I have seen her or not. She looks just like hundreds of other young women that come through here every week to put some excitement in their dreary lives."

Justin placed the photos he'd printed of the political candidates in front of the bartender and took over the interrogation. "How about one of these men? Ever seen either of them?"

"They both look familiar," Zeke admitted. "But that's all I can tell you."

"Familiar—you mean you've seen them *here* in this club?" Justin asked.

"Maybe," Zeke said evasively.

"Both of them?"

Zeke's expression darkened. "Look, I've told you what I can. What do you want from me, blood?"

"I want you to take a better look," Justin insisted. No doubt the bartender was trying to protect himself. "And I want the truth. Or I could let the NOPD ask you the same questions. I'm working closely with Mike Hebert, the detective in charge of the case."

Apparently the threat worked because Zeke said, "Okay, yeah, so I've seen them both."

"When was the last time they were here?"

"You got me."

"But you know who they are."

"Yeah, I watch the news occasionally," Zeke said. "But I don't keep track of who comes and who goes, or when and how often. This is a busy place, in case you haven't noticed. But I know for sure I haven't seen either one of them tonight. If you want to find one of these guys socially, check out the big shindig tomorrow night."

"What shindig would that be?" Lucy asked, seeming suddenly on alert.

"Big political fund-raiser, sponsored by some women's group. And that's all I know."

Not giving them a shot at another question, Zeke turned his back on them and made his way to a customer at the other end of the bar.

"Fund-raiser...political...an opportunity..." Justin said more to himself than to Lucy.

But she instantly responded, ''And I know how to make it happen.''

''Then why are we still here?'' he asked. ''Let's go someplace where we can talk about it.''

But the way out was blocked for the moment.

A woman on the dance floor held all watching her in thrall. She tossed her dark hair in a circle toward those in front of her, then did the same with her derriere to the crowd in back. Moans from most of the men—and from some of the women—rippled across the room.

Justin found himself pulling Lucy lightly to his side, and when she looked up at him, it was with hungry eyes. He was thinking how easy it would be to abandon the case and get one of those rooms upstairs when the music reached a crescendo as did the hot dance.

Then two men approached the dancer, each taking one arm. Onlookers stood in place, mesmerized by the struggle before them. Apparently each man expected the dancer to go with him. She ended the tug of war when she whispered something into one man's ear, then into the other's. The two men made up their minds and all three walked together to one of the alcoves and slipped inside. The woman gave the crowd a sexy smile before drawing the curtain closed with a snap.

Her words coming out in a breathless whoosh, Lucy said, ''That was some performance.''

One that had turned them both on, if he was any judge. Lucy's features had softened as had her body pressed along his side.

"Part of me wonders if it was real, though," he admitted, looking around at some of the activities that seemed to be marginally legal in public. "Or was this something arranged by management to inspire the crowd."

"You think anyone who comes to a club like this needs inspiration?"

He gave Lucy a heated gaze. "I have to admit I'm pretty inspired."

Her lips parted and her tongue darted out to wet them. Justin couldn't help himself—he leaned over to help, the touch of his tongue on her lips giving him a jolt that went straight to his dick. With a little moan that did him in, Lucy wrapped her arms around his neck and pressed her softness to his hard-on.

Knowing this was insane, Justin took her in his arms, began dancing her across the floor to the exit while indulging himself in a long, lust-filled kiss. He probed her hot mouth the way he would like to probe her body. Imagination running amuck, he thought of several ways they could do it, each making him hotter than the last until his hard-on had a hard-on.

His hands practically circled her waist. He slid them higher, under the top, and allowed his thumbs to glide along the side of her breasts. She was wearing a bra, but the material was so fine that he could feel the heat of her flesh through it—she might as well not be wearing anything at all.

Sighing into his mouth, she kept the kiss going while shifting her breasts away from his chest slightly, giving his thumbs room to maneuver. He touched her soft tips and used the pads of his thumbs to caress the nipples into hard, tight points that he yearned to take into his mouth and savor.

Realizing they'd reached the other side of the dance crowd, Justin came up for air and released her breasts. But everything was hazy, especially anything that didn't have to do with having Lucy as soon as possible.

"I want you," he said.

She nipped his lower lip. "Ditto."

For a moment, he was tempted to find out whether they did have rooms upstairs, but then he thought better of it. He didn't want to make love to her in a place like this, no matter how exciting it seemed.

He wanted her alone, all to himself, where no one could hear her cry out in response to his exquisite torture.

Justin pushed away the caution that had made him wait this long to have Lucy. What did it matter if they made love tonight or several nights from now? What if they never nailed the murderer and he kept his vow, which meant he would never have her at all. Unthinkable. And unnecessary.

Just because he'd let his hormones loose didn't mean he would be letting down his guard. He didn't intend to let Lucy out of his sight again until the case was solved.

With that resolved, he led her to the exit before one of them could change their mind.

IGNORING the No Parking sign—a man in his position could snap his fingers and any ticket would be forgiven—he left his car at the corner and headed down the block, anxious to get to the club. He'd stayed away long enough.

He probably shouldn't be indulging himself, not without a bodyguard, not with his race for reelection just starting in truth. But his bodyguards were busy keeping an eye out for Lucy Ryan, and his constituents had voted for him because he was a man's man. They would expect him to have certain…appetites.

This particular appetite quickly faded, however, when he saw someone who could be the Ryan woman herself slip out of the doorway with a man in tow. He immediately hugged the shadows lest they turn and see him.

He glared at them, willed her to turn so he could better see her face to be certain. As if on command, she did, glancing up at her companion. He kissed her and she lifted a leg and wrapped it around the back of his.

His groin tightened and he silently cursed. He'd needed the club tonight, but now he had something more important on his mind.

She was the Ryan woman, he was sure of it.

Racing back to his car, he figured to follow them. Since she'd abandoned her town house, that would be the only way he'd know where to find her.

Lucy Ryan had seen what he'd done. She was a liability, and he couldn't afford liabilities. That's how this whole mess had started. Not that anyone would believe he had actually murdered that tarot-reading whore.

But still, even the hint could ruin his chances of reelection.

Glancing back as he got to his car, he saw they were headed down the street, their hands all over each other. He got in the car and started to trail them.

He never should have gotten involved with anyone on more than a one-night stand basis. And certainly not with someone so unsophisticated. But he'd been taught by the best how wielding power over an innocent could be an aphrodisiac—he'd learned that from his own stepmother when he'd been a teenager—and Theresa had been a sweet conquest. It had been his pleasure not only to deflower her as she'd wanted, but to corrupt her, as well. He'd taken everything from her as everything had been taken from him.

Then she'd thought he was hers. As if he would give up everything—wife, children, home, profession—for a pretty little piece of ass. She'd threatened him, had said she would go to his wife to settle things....

He pulled to the curb when he saw the Ryan woman get into a car with the man. Then he waited until the lights went on and the car crawled off. Another car was coming, and for a moment, he feared he would lose them. But after a few blocks, the other car turned off. He could ride right up into their trunk if he so chose. He gripped the steering wheel so he wouldn't be tempted.

Patience. Everything came to the man who could

curb his impulses...ironically, something he should have done with Theresa Vaughn.

He followed them out of the French Quarter and into an area of loft conversions. Sure enough, Ryan's escort drove his car into a garage.

He noted the address and left the car long enough to write down the names of the tenants. Not that he would figure it out himself. He would leave that to his investigator and have an answer by the end of business the next day.

And then he would see to their quick demise.

FRENZIED BY the long wait she'd had for this moment, Lucy swept her tongue up Justin's hard length with a passion she hadn't ever before experienced. A passion that had finally taken over, not allowing her to back down, even knowing what she did.

Though she realized this was exactly what she'd been doing the first time she'd dreamed of Justin, she couldn't stop herself.

She would simply change it...not play out the sex dream as she'd dreamed it.

But first...she sucked the sweet softness of his head into her mouth, reveling in the drop of come that met her tongue. He moaned, and fingers of fire sluiced down her body to the heat between her thighs.

Oh, yes, she did want him there. And she would have him, at least for a bit.

Slowly, she eased herself upward, until their mouths met in a hot kiss.

He swallowed her whole with that kiss, making her feel as if she were drowning.

Too familiar...too familiar...now was the time to change things, Lucy thought hazily.

"Let's get in the shower and do it there with water beating down on us," she said, trying to get off the floor where they'd dropped their clothes in a frenzied rush.

"Later," Justin whispered, holding on to her, not letting her get away from him. "In the shower...in the ˙ed...on the washer, if you like. Anywhere you want ˙r. But right now, it's right here."

˙nd before she could protest, he was kissing her again and the tip of his erection probed at her hot center and she was lost. Not that her good intentions were forgotten. But she had to feel him inside her, at least for a bit. Then she would change things. She would insist she wanted to bring him off with her mouth and he would let her. He'd loved the things she'd done to him with her mouth.

She ended the kiss and pushed herself up so that she could see him. His sharp features were punctuated by a fall of inky hair across his high forehead. Watching them excited her, especially his eyes. Bedroom eyes with heavy lids that revealed the promise of pleasure...bedroom eyes that could make her insides curl.

Her insides were curling now.

"Stop!" she said.

He stopped. "Did I hurt you?"

"No, it all feels wonderful," she admitted, "but you know what would feel better?"

He seemed interested in this. "What?"

"I want you in my mouth." She licked her lips, adding, "I want to taste you, especially when you come."

"Later," he said.

She felt him moving under her, his hot hands slid along her thighs, then a thumb stroked her clit so sweetly she could hardly think. "This first. Oh, Lucille, I want you to come first. I want to watch your face when you can't stand it anymore. I want to come because you take me there with you."

Before she could gather the will to protest, to try to change his mind, his free hand traveled upward to her breasts. And then when he tugged at a nipple and stroked her clit in tandem, she was lost to sensation. She couldn't stop her back from arching or from opening herself wider to him.

Just like in the dream...

"Now, *chère,* now!"

She wanted to hold on long enough to stop him...to make the reality end differently than the dream...but he wouldn't ease up on her and the friction pushed her over the edge. The pulsing began deep inside her, and she dug her nails into the flesh of his thighs. He jerked and made a low guttural sound, and her murky world turned bright as they fell into the abyss together....

He held her close for a few moments, kissing the top of her head and her temples. Then he dipped lower and kissed her on the mouth, long and deep, and some-thing stirred against her belly, making her aware that he wasn't ready to call it a night.

"Justin..."

"Shh," he hushed her, as he scooped her up into his arms as if she weighed nothing and headed for the stairs.

She clung to him, not wanting to end this, knowing she should.

A moment later, he tumbled with her into his bed.

"I'm tired," she murmured, closing her eyes and hoping he would take the hint.

The second dream had taken place in this very bed.

"You rest, then," Justin said, kissing her lightly, now from her chin to her chest to her stomach.

Lucy deepened her breathing, tried to pretend she was asleep, but Justin wasn't buying it. He continued seducing her with his mouth and with his tongue. She began to squirm under him, then turned to crawl away.

He caught up to her as she grasped the iron bedstead to pull herself up.

"Mmm, just like that," he whispered, suddenly fit-ting himself behind her.

Oh, no, this was it. The second dream. He felt hot and heavy between her thighs and she could do noth-ing but draw him to her. She pooled wet and thick, a hot slick invitation he couldn't resist. Her hands tight-ened on the bedstead as he began to pulse behind her. She was on her knees, and he hooked his fingers into her hips so she tilted a bit. Then, her bottom pressed into his groin, he slid in and out of her and ran his hands over her body as if trying to memorize every inch.

When he had her where he wanted her, he slid a hand to her breasts, where he tugged her nipples until she cried out. His other hand explored lower, where it feathered her and then found her clit.

"There," she murmured as he slid a single finger along the sensitive area. "Oh, yes, sweet heaven…"

The dream…exactly as in the dream…

She glanced up to catch a reflection of them in the mirror. He watched her there, his bedroom eyes glittering at her. She wanted to tell him…stop him, but she couldn't stop herself.

A lust-filled, flushed-face wanton, her red hair wild and radiant stared back at her from the mirror. His features were equally taut with lust. Licking her lips, she rubbed her breast against his hand and pushed back hard. Their coming together over and over excited her further.

She let go of the bedstead and reached back with one hand, flexed her fingers and scraped her nails against his hard flesh, until he came undone. Waves of pleasure rippled through her, too, and the moment was so intense, Lucy wanted to cry. This really was the best sex ever.

Justin pulled her down to lay against him and wrapped his arms around her.

"I've been dreaming about doing that since I met you," he whispered, his breath laving her ear.

And then she wanted to cry for a very different reason. No matter that she'd tried, she hadn't been able to change the outcome of that first psychic dream of him.

What had she done?

Horrified, Lucy held Justin close to her and hoped she hadn't just sentenced him to death.

14

PLAGUED WITH GUILT, Lucy couldn't sleep. Justin didn't have that problem. Holding her close, he'd passed out and snored softly.

Then it had begun to rain, reminding her of the third dream—the very *next* dream to come true if they came in order. In her mind's eye, she'd seen him coming toward her, then a shot had rung out and he'd dropped to the wet pavement.

She remained against him as long as she could stand it, then wiggled her way off the bed and got dressed.

She couldn't let it happen.

Desperate, Lucy knew the only way of stopping his dream-death from becoming reality was to stop the murderer.

It was time to tap into this gift of hers. The gift she'd reluctantly accepted all her life. The gift that had seemed so innocent until she'd met Justin.

She couldn't let the man she loved be shot and maybe die.

Tears gathered in her eyes and she swiped them away with the back of her hand. Crying wouldn't help anything. She was stronger than that. And she had a power that most women didn't...that most people didn't. She simply had to channel it in the right direction.

Emile Poree had recognized the danger she was in and had told her to do it.

Gran had told her how.

Now it was up to her.

Lucy spread out the photos across the coffee table next to the couch where she would try to fall asleep.

Cahill...Montgomery...Theresa...

At first she was only going to concentrate on the men, but then she realized that they might lead her elsewhere if she didn't include the young woman at the center of the crimes.

She studied them all carefully, memorizing details of each of their faces. Then she stared at Theresa, Gran's words echoing through her head.

Before you go to sleep, concentrate on the question...if your will is strong enough, your dream will give you the answer....

Her will had to be strong enough to prevent anything from happening to Justin.

"Tell me what I need to know," she demanded in a whisper. "What happened to you, Theresa?"

She silently repeated the question and stared at the photos until they began to blur. Exhausted, she turned off the light, slid down into a prone position on the couch, closed her eyes and concentrated.

She could see Theresa's face.

She could see them all.

They were burned into her memory.

What happened to you...what happened to you...what happened to you...?

The question rolled around and around in her mind before sleep finally claimed her.

THE RHYTHMIC THUMP-THUMP *of music called to her from where she waited in the dark, feeling as if she could affect what might happen next...and yet not.*

Whatever was happening felt different, out of her experience.

She was aware....

Thinking she must be back at the sex club, she steeled herself for whatever might come next. If she ran into the killer, surely he would recognize her, maybe try to kill her, too.

But what choice did she have? She had to take that chance.

She stepped into the light...flashing lights revealing a club of a different sort. Dancers here wore white-face and elaborate disguises...hair and costumes black or purple or bloodred.

A Goth club. What the hell was she doing here?

She swept across the dance floor, looking for a familiar face. The one she caught sight of was totally unexpected.

"Jenn!"

But her sister was across the room and obviously couldn't hear her. She was frowning as she argued with another young Goth.

This didn't make sense.

"Jenn!" she called again, but the music was ear-piercing and her voice was lost in it.

Frustrated, she fought through the gyrating crowd to get to her sister, but just as she was about to reach her—

A hand shook her shoulder.

"Lucy, wake up."

Her eyes opened to see Justin staring down at her with an expression of concern.

She had failed.

Though she had tried to make her dream go where she wanted, it had gone where it would.

"Oh, Justin!" she cried, sitting up and throwing her arms around his neck.

"Bad dream?"

"Sort of."

She shuddered against him. She was so disappointed that she wanted to weep. She'd failed miserably to protect him. What was she going to do?

"Hey, it's okay," he told her, rubbing her back with one hand. "I'm here now."

Indeed he was.

But for how long?

LUCY SEEMED TO RELAX a little after having some hot tea, which Justin had insisted on fixing for her. Though he wanted to know what had frightened her, he gave her a few minutes of breathing room.

He finally checked his messages—which paid off with a name and address of Mr. Shoe Fetish Phil Beatty. He scribbled the information down on a pad.

"Phil Beatty," Lucy repeated. "What are you going to do with that information?"

"Give it to Mike."

"For which he'll thank you very much and tell you to butt out again."

"Probably. That doesn't mean I will," Justin said, joining Lucy, who was pouring herself another cup of tea. He sat on the couch next to her, saying, "So tell me what's wrong."

"Why would you think something is wrong?" she asked, her voice sounding tense.

"Because you're not yourself. Because you weren't in bed next to me when I woke up looking for you."

"I couldn't sleep."

"Talk, Lucy. Until you do, I won't let you out of here."

He was joking, but truth be told, Justin was ready to keep her and not let her go anyway. They hadn't even known each other for a week, but he felt he knew her better than anyone. Not to mention that he was crazy about her....

Looking torn, Lucy said, "What if you don't believe me?" in a tone so quiet she might have been talking to herself.

He leaned across the counter and took her hand. "Does this have to do with the dream you had?"

She nodded. "Among others."

"Well, we won't know if I'm a believer until you tell me."

Her eyes serious round pools of gray, she gazed at him steadily. "It started right before I met you."

"You're talking about the dream where Sophie was murdered."

"No, not that one. After…in the motel…I had another one…about you."

"Me? You mean before you met me?" he asked, trying to keep the skepticism out of his voice. He still wasn't sure what to believe when it came to Lucy's psychic dreams. "What kind of dream?"

"What we did here on the floor last night."

He relaxed. "An erotic dream?"

She nodded. "The first of several. What we did upstairs we did in dream number two."

"Sounding good to me, *chère*," Justin said, grinning at her. "So why are you upset?"

"The first two dreams have come true. If the third one does…" She shuddered. "That's why I was trying to stretch my gift. I talked to Gran about it and she said I could do it if only I concentrated hard enough."

"Whoa, you've lost me here."

"Before I went to sleep, I concentrated on photographs of Cahill and Montgomery and Theresa. I wanted to find out what happened to Theresa, so I concentrated on that, made that my focus as I fell asleep. But it didn't do any good. Instead of seeing what happened to Theresa, I dreamed about my sister Jenn at a Goth club."

Though he wanted to laugh, Justin kept it in. Lucy took her dreams seriously and wouldn't appreciate his being amused by them. "That's what has you so upset?"

"Not exactly. I wanted to latch on to something that would help us catch the murderer…and save *you*."

His grin faded. "Save me from what?"

"From getting shot. The third dream. I heard a shot ring out and then you dropped to the pavement—"

"You dreamed someone shot me?"

She nodded and tears pooled in her eyes. "Because of me."

"I prefer the erotic dreams."

"You're not taking me seriously."

"I take you very seriously, Lucille." He moved in closer and stroked the side of her face. "Why don't we see if we can fulfill the next erotic dream?"

"Justin, stop." Lucy squirreled away from him to the end of the couch. "If we don't find a way to stop it from happening, you're going to be shot."

"No, I won't."

"How can you say that after what I just told you?"

"It was a dream, *chère*."

"It was one of *my* dreams."

"Has every dream you've ever had come true?"

"The psychic dreams have."

"How do you know which is which?" he asked. "Maybe this was just a plain old dream, and you were jazzed by the trouble you were in."

Her expression turned to one of disbelief. "I thought you believed me. If you didn't believe me about seeing Sophie murdered in a dream, why did you go along with me?"

"There were real murderers after you, Lucy. I was there when they tried to kill you."

"But you don't believe I saw Sophie die in a dream?"

Justin didn't want to upset her, but he didn't want to lie to her, either.

"I'm not sure what to believe when it comes to any of the psychic stuff."

"I can't believe this." Bounding to her feet, saying, "I thought you were different," Lucy's knee knocked knee into the cup, sending tea over the table.

When she righted the cup and grabbed napkins, he took them from her. "I'll get this. Sit down and relax."

But Lucy backed away from the couch and looked at him as if she were seeing him for the first time.

And not liking what she was seeing.

"*Chère,* relax, already, please." Now *he* was getting tense. He swabbed at the tea and added, "Let's talk about this." Not that he really wanted to.

"There's nothing to talk about."

When he looked up, Lucy was already at the door. "Hey, where are you going?"

"Away from you. Believe or don't believe. I won't be responsible for you getting shot."

Before he could think of a response that would change her mind, she was out the door. Justin bounded up from the couch and went after her, but she kept a step ahead of him. The elevator whirred as it took her down to the ground floor.

And out of his life?

DOWN AT STREET LEVEL, Lucy tried to get a taxi, but it was raining, and none were to be found.

So she jogged over to Charles Street and lucked out. Within minutes, a all-night streetcar crawled up out of the Garden District. A few others rode the line with her to the edge of the French Quarter. Thankfully, when she got off, the rain had let up, and she could walk the rest of the way home.

How had she been so wrong about Justin? She'd thought he believed her and accepted her, psychic dreams and all. Now it seemed that he was no different than the other men she'd let into her life for brief periods of time. She and Justin were connected by the murders, but once the killer was nailed, he'd probably disappear right out of her life, just like the others had.

If he was still alive, that was.

When she was more than halfway through the French Quarter, the rain started up again. She sped up as the mournful sounds of a saxophone drifted through the wet night. Some people were still out, but not many. The late action was over on Bourbon Street. Even a torrent wouldn't stop the barhoppers who were determined to make every moment in the French Quarter count.

Lucy could care less that she was soaking. She didn't even know how she was holding herself together, keeping herself from crying.

She couldn't wait for the privacy of her own bedroom.

When she was within a block from the town house, she heard a splash behind her. Heart thudding, she turned to look. Nothing. Hearing the sound of laughter, then moans, she pressed her hands to her ears and ran.

Suddenly, she realized this was it—the start of the third dream. She flew down the wet street. She slowed when she neared the courtyard, but her pulse was still racing.

"Don't be there," she prayed, pulling her keys out of her pocket.

But he was.

The moment Lucy stepped into the courtyard, she saw Justin, rivulets of rain sheening his face. For a moment, she faltered and stared, tears welling in her eyes once more.

"What are you doing here?" she demanded, whirling around, searching the shadows for the man with the gun. "Get out or you'll be shot!"

But before Justin could answer, a sharp blast came from behind her, and she turned to see Justin's body jerk from the impact.

"No!" Lucy screamed, watching in horror as the man she loved crumpled to the wet flagstone as if in slow motion.

"Hey, what's going on?" yelled a man across the street.

"I'm calling the police!" yelled another.

Lucy heard this from afar, as if she were disconnected from her body. In the time it took her to get to Justin, she heard the slap-slap of feet running and an engine rev as a car shot down the street.

"Justin, oh, J-Justin, I tr-tried to warn you," Lucy sobbed. As she sank to her knees beside him, he moaned, and the knot in her stomach loosened. "You're alive!"

Justin opened his eyes, gasped as he tried to suck in some air.

"Don't try to talk. You're alive!" she sobbed, adding, "I'll get an ambulance."

"No, not…wounded," he said with another gasp and a moan for good measure.

That stopped her from leaving his side. "What?"

"Wearing…bulletproof vest," he gritted out. "Just my…breath…knocked out of me."

As the sound of police sirens drew closer and a flashing light pierced the courtyard, a relief like none she'd ever felt before washed through her. She hadn't killed him, after all. Thankfully, Dana had been right, and Lucy didn't know whether to laugh or cry.

Justin was all right, and for the moment, that's all that mattered.

15

BEFORE JUSTIN even gave the uniformed officer his statement, he asked that Detective Mike Hebert be called in on the case. Though the detective grumbled about being roused from his bed, he arrived at Lucy's town house within the half hour.

After glancing at the officer's report and bidding the man a good-night, Mike said, "You reported the how and when. What I expect are the whys and wherefores."

Wincing when he moved too fast—while the vest might have saved him from being shot, it didn't save him from a hell of a bruise—Justin said, "It's all there."

"If it were all here, I'm assuming you wouldn't have gotten me out of bed."

Which was true. Justin had wanted another try at getting Mike to cooperate. Surely now he would see that working together would be in everyone's best interest.

So he asked, "Does the name Phil Beatty ring any bells for you?"

"Can't say that it does."

Justin glanced at Lucy, expecting to feel her disapproval, but she hardly seemed aware of what was going on. Apparently she was still freaked by the shooting, and he realized the incident had affected her more negatively than it had him. After expressing her gratitude at finding he was alive, she'd hardly said a word other than answering direct questions.

Turning back to Mike, Justin said, "Beatty may have been the shooter tonight."

"What makes you think so?"

"He's been involved from the first. He was there when Sophie Delacorte was killed."

"And you know this how?"

"Because I saw him," Lucy said, finally coming to life. "He and his buddy tried to kill me to keep me quiet."

"You witnessed the Delacorte woman's murder?" Mike said, his voice raising a notch.

"Not exactly."

"What then?"

Justin didn't say a word. It was up to Lucy to reveal her psychic abilities.

But she merely said, "Sophie had already been stabbed by the time I got there," avoiding mentioning the dream altogether. "I saw them standing over her body. The man holding the knife wore a hat, so I never saw his face."

"I see," Mike said. "So you didn't feel it important enough to tell me that much before?"

"Lucy would have, but I convinced her otherwise." Justin's protective instincts kicked into gear. "I thought she would be safest if we gathered as much information as we could before she came forward. You know you don't have the resources to keep her safe.''

Mike looked as if he wanted to spit nails, but he kept his anger under control and focused on Lucy. ''I think you need to come to the station so we can get all this down in an official statement.''

Lucy nodded her agreement, so that's what they did.

But once at the station, never once in her story did Lucy admit to having psychic dreams. Considering the way he'd reacted earlier, Justin couldn't blame her.

Before they left the station, Mike had all the solid details: how two men had tracked Lucy to bayou country…how Justin had decided to come back to New Orleans to help her…how they'd followed Mr. Shoe Fetish from the club to get his license plate number and therefore his identity.

In return, Mike merely told them the department computer geek was still working on Theresa's laptop. He also said he would get someone on Phil Beatty's trail and that he would have someone stake out Lucy's place in case Beatty or his pal came back for another try at her.

By the time they left the station, it was morning and the city was awake.

Newspaper headlines indicated the woman murdered in the courtyard was Sophie Delacorte, tarot reader. So now the whole city knew.

Lucy remained reserved over breakfast, but she announced her intention of visiting her parents' home. ''If anyone has the inside track on that political fundraiser tonight, my mother does.''

Her voice tightened slightly when she mentioned her mother, and Justin got the impression that things didn't always run smoothly between the two women.

"I'll come with you, if that's all right."

"If that's what you choose to do."

Her words were softly spoken yet had a sharp edge to them. He wasn't going to be able to dismantle the wall between them so easily. At least she wasn't trying to cut him out of her life completely.

Not that Justin would let her.

But for the moment, he would defer to her, give her some room to bounce back from their argument and the trauma she'd suffered that morning.

Surely she would.

When they arrived in the Garden District, Justin was taken aback by the obvious wealth of Lucy's family. She was so down-to-earth, had such a strong work ethic, he never would have expected her to have grown up in one of the area's finest mansions.

"Would you tell my mother I'm here?" Lucy asked the woman who answered the door.

"Yes, Miss."

A servant, Justin thought. Of course servants went with the territory, but to him it seemed odd that Lucy would have to go through a servant to see her own mother. Maybe it seemed odd to her, too, the reason her voice had gone tight when she'd spoken of her mother earlier.

Feeling like a bull in a china shop, he followed Lucy into a large antique-filled parlor with a crystal chandelier and a fireplace big enough to roast a pig.

"This is some place."

"Mama loves it."

"But you don't?"

"I love it for the history it represents—including that of our family—but I wouldn't choose a place like this for myself. Not that I could ever afford to run it. Well, not unless I chose to open my trust fund."

A trust fund. Of course. One she obviously wasn't into spending. He could see that about Lucy. She was probably one of the most self-reliant women he'd ever known. She would want to make her own way, not depend on someone else's success. And yet, she wasn't running on full throttle.

Thinking of her so-far-unrecognized talent and the reasons why that was so, he said, "You never know what could happen if you started believing in yourself."

That made her look at him directly. A shadow marred her soft gray eyes when she asked, "What makes you think I don't believe in myself?"

"My first clue was that you don't feature your own masks in your shop...my second was that you don't trust other people enough to tell them the whole truth."

Her so-called gift clearly was the source of her insecurity.

"Right," she muttered, "and look what happens when I am honest."

"If you were comfortable with your psychic dreams, you wouldn't let the fact that others doubt them or try to belie them bother you so much."

Justin wanted to say a whole lot more, but Lucy was wearing an expression only a tad warmer than the one that had been glued to her face all morning.

Then heels clicked across the marble vestibule floor, and Justin turned to see a sleek brunette who was probably in her early fifties but appeared a decade younger. Her dress was a deep blue number with a cut-out at one shoulder—dramatically simple as was her silver cuff bracelet studded with a single large sapphire a shade darker than her eyes.

Kat Ryan looked nothing like her daughter, and their styles were as different as could be. While he registered the fine appearance of the mother, Justin didn't think she was a match for her more down-to-earth daughter.

Then, again, he knew he was prejudiced since he couldn't imagine a woman lovelier than Lucy.

"Lucy, darlin', you should have called to let me know you were coming." Kat took Lucy's hand and lightly touched a cheek to her daughter's, then eyed him. "And who might this gentleman be?"

"Mama, this is Justin Guidry, a private investigator."

She couldn't even introduce him as a friend, making Justin realize how angry and disappointed in him Lucy remained.

"Oh, my, is there something I should be worrying about?"

"No, Mama, relax," Lucy said. "Justin is working on this case and I said possibly you could help him."

"My, this sounds important. Would you like something cool and refreshing to drink, Mr. Guidry?"

"I'm fine."

"Well, let's sit then, shall we?"

Justin found himself perched on a spindly legged chair and hoping it was strong enough to hold him.

"Now how can I help you?" Kat Ryan asked.

He said, "We understand there's a big political fund-raiser in New Orleans tonight and were wondering if you could tell us more about it."

"The Daughters of Fine Lineage is sponsoring A Touch of Magic to help finance the coming election."

"Mama is one of the 'Daughters' and is probably head of some committee or other."

"Invitations."

"Really," Justin said, looking to use the opportunity to their best advantage. "Does that mean you can invite anyone you want?"

"Of course."

"Then how about us?" Lucy asked, picking up on his idea. "Can you spare two tickets?"

Her mother's eyes widened. "So that you can ruin the event with your investigation—"

"Mama, this is important to me. Please."

Kat Ryan seemed startled, Justin thought, almost as if her daughter had never asked her for a favor before. Which perhaps she hadn't. Lucy was probably a bit too independent for her own good.

"Perhaps you'd better tell me something about this case of yours," Kat said.

"Can't you do this one thing for me without negotiating?"

Her mother frowned. A moment passed before she agreeably said, "All right, Lucy, I'll get you both in if that's what you want."

"Thank you. Tell us about the event."

"Drinks and appetizers and entertainment will be followed by a formal dinner."

"What kind of entertainment?" Lucy asked.

"Psychics, of course—the event is called A Touch of Magic," she reminded them. "We'll have tarot and palm readers and astrologers. That sort of thing."

While her mother continued to talk, Lucy withdrew. He noticed she glanced several times toward the foyer which fronted a parlor on the opposite side.

"Is something bothering you, darlin'?" Kat suddenly asked her daughter.

Lucy seemed to come to. "I'm sorry. I was simply wondering if Daddy was home this morning."

"He's in his study."

"I need to talk to him about something. Do either of you mind?"

"No, go ahead. I'm sure Mr. Guidry has more questions."

Lucy was already on her feet. "I'll be back in a few minutes."

Justin watched her head out of the room and make a sharp right on the other side of the stairs.

"Now I wonder what that's all about."

He noted the surprise in her mother's voice. It seemed that Lucy had been dead-on in her evaluation of her family dynamics. She apparently *wasn't* at all close to her parents, and her interest in her father surprised her mother as much as everything else that had gone on since they'd arrived.

Kat turned back to him, her expression concerned. "My daughter isn't in some kind of trouble, is she?"

"She hasn't done anything wrong," Justin said evasively, cheered that at least the woman seemed to care about Lucy.

"Thank goodness. I worry about that girl." Kat shook her head and asked, "Now, what else do you need to know, Mr. Guidry?"

Justin easily got her to talk in more detail about the fund-raiser—from the way the rooms of the old mansion would be set up to specifics about the companies providing catering and entertainment.

But all the while he was wondering what was going on between Lucy and her father.

SILVER-HAIRED, Jack Ryan had a reputation for being a gentleman with a sugar tongue and a steel will that had made him the success he'd been his entire adult life. He'd taken his father's business and had expanded it until Ryan Cartage International owned more warehouses in ports from New Orleans north along the Mississippi River than any other company.

Lucy had always wondered if his success was strictly due to a combination of hard work and luck...or if he'd inherited some aspect of his mother's gift that he'd never revealed.

Whatever the source, his zealous attention to business had left Lucy and Jenn fatherless for a good part of their lives. He'd been there on holidays and birthdays, but not so much in between—no doubt the reason their mother Kat had become a social matron at too early an age. She'd had to find something to do with the time on her hands.

Yet Lucy had always trusted that her father would come through for her if push came to shove, and the proposal she'd just presented was his test.

"I don't like this, Lucy, girl," he said, his gray eyes so like her own filled with worry, "but if you're set on it—"

"I am, Daddy." She'd told him everything—well, nearly—and had asked for his cooperation. "I need your help so no one gets hurt."

"What about the police?"

"We've given the detective in charge as much information as possible, but he's not going to approve this kind of sting operation. He won't do anything with so many influential people around. He needs proof and I intend to give it to him. I can't live with this, Daddy." She could die with it, but she continued to leave that part out. "I saw Sophie Delacorte killed in a dream for a reason—so that I could help catch her murderer."

He thought for a moment, then nodded. "All right, then. I'll do as you ask. I'll talk to your mama and make the arrangements."

"Don't frighten her, please."

"You can't keep protecting her, Lucy. You and your sister have been dancing around the fact that you're both different since you were children. Kat knows. She's your mother and she feels your burden even if she tries to hide it.''

So they'd all spent a lifetime pretending. ''Thank you for believing in me.''

She did believe in herself, no matter what Justin thought. That's why she was taking matters into her own hands.

''I've always believed in you, Lucy, girl,'' her father said, his voice rich with pride. ''You're like me. A self-starter. That's why I wanted to bring you into the business, so that a Ryan would always be at the helm.''

''I have to make my own way, Daddy. I'm sure you understand that.''

She wouldn't tell him that she hated the business that had stolen her father from her, and if he left the company to her in his will, she would sell her shares in Ryan Cartage Intercontinental and give every penny away. No way would she duplicate the life he'd built for himself to the detriment of her own family.

If she ever had her own family...

Now why couldn't she see *that* in one of her dreams?

''Tonight,'' her father said, ''promise me you will be careful.''

''Daddy, didn't you always say I was the sensible daughter?''

''That's not an answer.''

''It's the best one I have.''

''Then it'll do for now.''

Her father enfolded her in his arms and the moment made her eyes sting. Why did it have to take a situation like this to bring out his affection for her? But when he released her, Lucy made sure she was smiling.

"Tonight, then," she said, heading for the door.

Before exiting, she glanced back, but her father was already concentrating on the morning newspaper again.

He would come through for her.

He had to.

Justin and Mama were waiting for her in the foyer. Mama looked as if she wanted to know what had gone on in the study, but as usual, she didn't ask.

"Ready?" Lucy asked Justin.

"Ready if you are. Your mother gave me the tickets."

Lucy offered her cheek to Mama, expecting the usual light brush, but instead received a kiss and then a nervous brush of fingers over her cheek.

"Lipstick," Mama explained.

Lucy wanted to tell her that it was all right, that she could leave the lipstick, but a lump in her throat got in her way.

"I'll see you tonight," she mumbled.

Impulsively kissing her mother's cheek in return, Lucy was out the door before she could feel any awkwardness over the affectionate gesture. For once, she felt like she had the full backing of both her parents and was a little breathless.

She was even feeling softer toward Justin. He hadn't abandoned her…yet.

They were in the car before he said, "So we have a start. We have the invitations to get us into the fund-raiser. Now all we need is to figure out how to determine which of our suspects is guilty."

"I have an idea about how to do that," Lucy admitted. "Let's get over to Jackson Square and see if we can find Emile Poree."

"Emile?"

"He may be able to get me a gig as a tarot reader at the party."

"And you want to do this why?"

"To catch a murderer, of course."

She didn't want to elaborate further until they found Emile. Justin dropped her off at the edge of Jackson Square and went to find parking.

The psychic was already at work with a client, but he saw her standing to the side and indicated he wanted to speak to her. She easily bribed Emile away from an already active crowd with a café au lait and beignets at Café du Monde. The place was busy, despite the clouds threatening more rain. Justin arrived just as they did. Luckily, they could be seated right away.

Once they got settled and gave the waitress their orders, Emile asked, "So what is it I can do for you?" His gaze was penetrating. "I told you all I could about Sophie."

Lucy nodded. "Now how would you like to help us catch her killer?"

"Say the word."

"Yes, say several," Justin said. "What kind of a scheme have you come up with?"

"The fund-raiser tonight—A Touch of Magic. I need to be hired as a tarot reader." She gave Emile a pleading look. "Can you make it happen?"

"I know the woman who has the contract."

Emile pulled out a cell phone and made a call. He spoke fast, weaving a good deal of patois into the conversation. From it, Lucy gathered he invoked Sophie's murder to convince her. No doubt anyone tied to the psychic community would want to see that it was solved.

Emile finished his call and said, "Done."

Their café au lait and beignets arrived in the midst of his giving her the details.

Justin asked, "How do you plan to pull this off? You do have a plan, right?"

"A pretty good one, I hope," Lucy said. "If you remember, Odette told us that Sophie bought the bordello deck for an important client. I'm guessing our murderer is that very client. Maybe I can figure out a way to get him to talk while reading his cards."

"If he indulges," Emile said.

"He will, especially if he sees a bordello deck."

"You actually think Mike will turn those cards over to us?" Justin asked, his voice rich with disbelief.

"No. But I have some talent, enough to whip up a facsimile that'll pass."

"How, when you don't have the original cards?"

"Famous decks have been photographed," Emile said.

Lucy added, "There's more than one Web site with hundreds of images."

"But what if we can't find Lamar Landrieu's work?"

"Then I'll improvise. Sophie had the deck on her when she died, which leaves me to believe she used it to read the murderer's tarot that night. What if I read Sophie's death in the cards?"

Emile said, "You're playing a dangerous game."

"One I don't like," Justin added.

"I've been playing a dangerous game from the first dream." Lucy met Justin's gaze, knowing that no matter how he felt about her gift, she could count on him to protect her. "But this time I'll have you to back me up."

16

AFTER PARTING from Emile, Lucy and Justin walked to a nearby voodoo shop where she picked up a tarot deck with a black background and simple design that could be painted over. Then they went straight to Bal Masque where Lucy quickly explained to Dana the basics of their project.

In the rear room, she cleared a table used to make their masks. At the computer, Justin found a picture of the famous bordello deck online and printed a copy she could use as a guide.

Handing her the print of a nearly nude woman hanging off an iron-lace balcony of a bordello, Justin said, "Too bad I don't have an artistic bent."

"You're good for other things."

"I am, am I? Care to elaborate?"

He was trying to act like there was nothing wrong between them. Truth be told, Lucy didn't want there to be anything between them. Not that she could forget the excitement and depth of their lovemaking, but she had to put that out of her mind.

It was important that she get through the next twelve hours without putting them in more danger than necessary, so she decided for the moment it would be best to let go of her disappointment in Justin concerning her gift. She had to pretend that nothing was wrong, that he wouldn't walk out of her life once this case was solved.

Lucy handed Justin a brush and tube of black acrylic. "Your strokes are flawless."

"You want me to paint you?"

The way he said it—as in paint her body—triggered a response in her that Lucy tried to ignore.

"The cards!" she said. "Give the design a light go-over." She turned on a ceiling fan to help dry the cards without moving them. She also had a quick-dry spray that would help. "I'll follow you and do a figure in flesh, then you follow me with some swirls around the edges with gold. Then I'll do another pass and fill in any missing details."

She indicated what she meant in the printout.

"Got it."

Justin was giving her a hungry look that made Lucy's knees weak.

"Let's get started," she mumbled, sorting tubes while he spread out the cards like an assembly line.

As they worked together, she once again thought they made a great team. He wanted her to believe in herself. Well, too bad he didn't believe in her.

A couple of hours later, they were done and Lucy was satisfied.

"Great job," Dana said, joining them between customers.

"You really think they'll do?"

"You could have been an art forger if you had a bent in that direction."

Lucy glanced at Justin, who was grinning at Dana's comment, then said, "Well, good. Hopefully they'll fool the murderer long enough to get him to incriminate himself. Now all I have to do is figure out how to keep him from recognizing me."

"Wear one of those headdresses and lots of makeup," Dana suggested.

Lucy sighed. "I don't own a lot of makeup."

"Your sister Jennifer does," Justin said.

"Jenn…yes, she does, doesn't she?"

Which might explain why she'd dreamed about her sister, Lucy thought. With Jenn's help, their own mother wouldn't recognize her!

"MAYBE WE SHOULD have gone back to see Odette," Justin said.

In the midst of their preparations for that night's work, Justin was gathering electronic equipment in a discreet leather bag.

"Why? Do you think the voodoo queen will be there tonight?"

"Maybe she can make a protection potion."

Opening the yellow pages to tuxedo rentals, Lucy said, "You don't believe in things like potions."

"I need to be convinced," he said.

Lucy gave him a look before placing her call. She paced the loft as she spoke to the clerk. Luckily the shop had a rental that would fit him.

"You're all set," she said, realizing Justin had wandered off toward the counter. He had something in his hand. "What's that?"

"Proof. Or not."

"What?"

He jiggled the vial at her. "Odette's love potion."

Her heart began to thud. This scenario was unfamiliar. Not one of her dreams. She wasn't sure how to react.

But when Justin got close to her, warming her with his heat, and asked, "Well, ready to prove a point?" she sighed wistfully and knew whatever happened next would come naturally.

How could she turn him down?

"That love potion was for you, if you'll remember."

He handed her the vial and began stripping. He was challenging her. But she wasn't up to a challenge. Not tonight. Tonight she felt…well, odd. Wistful. Anxious. Confused.

"I need you tonight, *chère*," he murmured as he stood before her gloriously naked. "We need each other. Together we can do anything."

Mesmerized by his voice, knowing that he was right and fearing that tonight might be the final climax of their personal relationship, she opened the vial. Tipping it, she dripped fragrant oil down his stomach and along his shaft. She used her fingertips to rub the potion exactly where it was created to work.

Justin moaned and filled her hand, and slowly she began moving her fingers along his length. He closed his eyes and sighed, then reached out blindly for her.

She'd showered and was wearing his robe. He didn't remove it, merely parted it so he could find her and touch her and enter her. He did so with her back pressed against a support. And when he was deep inside her, he urged her legs up and around his back. She surrendered completely and let him make love to her for what seemed like forever.

And after he flooded her with his essence, he stayed inside her, and within minutes was hard enough to make sure she came.

Collapsing against him, she murmured in his ear, "So what do you think about the potion? Does it work or not?"

"Let me show you," he whispered, then began moving inside her again.

"JUST PUTTING ON a lot of makeup doesn't make you a Goth," Jenn said, sitting Lucy down in front of her makeup table.

"I don't actually want to become a Goth, I just want to look like one."

Lucy had explained to Jenn the basics of what was going on—not revealing, of course, that men were after her. Her sister was reluctantly going along with the plan. Justin had dropped her off at the cottage on Magazine Street that Jenn had bought with her trust fund—her sister didn't have the same problems using the family money that Lucy did. Jenn had bought a small house and a few nice antiques and had given herself a modest monthly income that took her through the tough times when she couldn't get work.

After leaving her there, Justin had gone on to pick up that rental tuxedo. They would make some pair if they walked into that party together...which of course they wouldn't now.

"Smear this all over," Jenn said, handing Lucy a jar of skin cream. "Face, neck, shoulders, arms. It'll help get the makeup off later."

Doing as commanded, Lucy glanced at her sister in the mirror. Jenn was not only free of makeup at the moment, she wasn't even wearing a dark color. She looked so much like Mama right now, though Lucy dared not say it. Jenn would hate the comparison. Though she did use the Ryan money, Jenn wanted to be thought of as an individual, not seen as one member of a wealthy family. She just hadn't decided who it was she wanted to be yet, Lucy thought sardonically.

As Jenn applied the first coat of makeup, Lucy asked, "How come you're not Goth today?"

"Too much hassle if I'm not going anywhere. No work, plus I don't feel like clubbing tonight."

"Speaking of clubs...I dreamed about your being at one last night."

"I was." Jenn frowned at her. "One of *those* dreams?"

"I expect so. I can't seem to close my eyes lately without having a psychic episode."

"Why did you dream about *me*?" Jenn asked, sounding a little freaked, undoubtedly since Lucy had told her about seeing Sophie's murder. "What happened?"

"I don't know why. I was concentrating on someone else before I fell asleep, but there you were. I was trying to get to you, but you were too far away, and you were having a disagreement with another Goth girl.''

"Tess? Yeah, she took off on her own, and I was trying to convince her to go home and make up with her parents. She ought to let her parents, who love her, help her get out of trouble.''

"Right.''

Lucy could relate to that. Their parents had agreed to help her when she'd asked. Maybe she ought to loosen up and ask for things—personal time, for one— more often.

"But that's creepy,'' Jenn was saying, "you seeing me in dreams.''

"Not creepy,'' Lucy said, suddenly feeling a little creeped out herself. "I needed your help, and here I am.''

"Yeah. Well close your eyes and hold your breath so I can powder you down.''

Lucy obeyed and soon wanted to scratch her nose. How could Jenn stand putting this stuff on day after day? She held her breath until the powdering was over.

"So what about this Justin?'' Jenn asked. "Did you use the love potion?''

"That was a joke.''

"Humor is built on truth.'' Jenn was already applying a second coat of white to Lucy's face and neck. "So how hot is he?''

Lucy felt her ears burn and hoped it was embarrassment rather than the makeup. "Hot.''

''You did the deed?''

''Mostly in dreams.''

''Whoa, a qualifier.'' Jenn added more white to Lucy's shoulders, asking, ''Does that mean in reality, too? Details!''

''Not on your life.''

''C'mon. I'm starved for sex talk.''

''Sex talk or sex?'' Lucy asked.

''Both.''

''What happened to Chip What's-his-name?''

''The Chipper went North. Literally. Said he couldn't stand the heat.''

''New Orleans or you?''

''Probably both.'' Jenn sighed, and stopped applying for a moment. ''He told me I was too intense.''

''Argh.''

''Yeah, argh. That's why I've decided to become celibate for the foreseeable future.''

''Celibacy is overrated.''

''I won't know until I try it.''

Lucy laughed and Jenn did, too. No matter their different lifestyles, they were still sisters, still as close as they had been when they were kids. They could tell each other anything. Almost. Lucy had left out the part about the thugs coming after her and about being shot. She didn't want to worry Jenn more than necessary.

''Gran told me Justin was the one because of the dreams. She basically indicated that since I couldn't get him out of my mind, I wasn't going to get him out of my heart.''

''Was she right?''

"About the heart part?" Lucy swallowed hard and gave her sister the truth she'd been trying not to face. "Afraid so."

"Afraid so? You're in love and you don't want to be?"

"I thought Justin was different. About the gift, I mean. I thought he believed me…but he doesn't, not really."

"And you think that's weird?" Jenn smacked her lightly on top of her head. "Get real, Lucy. Who the heck is going to embrace what they can't understand? Why do you think I decided to stop listening when I got a premonition? Eventually they went away. So I don't have to deal with that particular problem."

Jenn spoke with all the fervor of a convert, but Lucy figured her sister was fooling herself. Sooner or later, Jenn would have to deal with her own gift, and it could be all the more intense for having denied it all these years.

"Give Justin a chance, Lucy. He hasn't walked away. He seems crazy about you."

Lucy flushed. Indeed he did, but hot sex was short-term. Truth be told, she was ready for commitment. Something she hadn't even known about herself until Justin. Then, she'd never been in love before.

"Maybe if you just blocked those dreams of yours, everything would be okay."

"No, it wouldn't be okay, not when I would be denying a part of myself."

Not wanting to think about how things were going to work out between them—that tonight might be the last time she even saw him—Lucy turned the conversation back on Jenn. And Jenn seemed grateful for the turn in topic. No doubt she didn't want to think about how she'd been denying *herself.*

The time flew as they teased each other about men and sex and before Lucy knew it, she became transformed from the Lucy that guys liked as a friend to a Lucille they might actually lust over…or perhaps fear just a little.

"Yikes, I don't even recognize myself."

"That's good, then," Jenn said with a laugh. "But one shower and you'll be yourself again."

Too bad, Lucy thought, imagining how Justin would react when he saw her.

WHEN JUSTIN STOPPED by the cottage on Magazine, a Goth girl who wasn't Jenn met him at the door.

"Lucy?" he asked doubtfully.

"Call me Lucille," she said in a deep, throaty whisper that turned him on.

Having fantasies wasn't hard just looking at her: white skin, black-ringed eyes, blood red-lips and nails and black hair straightened into a satin cloud. Her cleavage above the lace-up black vinyl bustier was damn impressive.

He practically salivated thinking about tonguing a nipple free of the material.

The rest of her was packaged nicely, also, in a clingy calf-length skirt. Too bad about the thick-soled combat boots, though at least she could run in them if she had to. Or break someone's leg by kicking it.

"So what do you think?" Lucy asked, turning for him.

He didn't want to think that either could happen or he would change his mind fast. He would be there and keep her safe. He would hear every word she said to every man who used her services. He would be on guard.

"I think your own mother wouldn't recognize you."

"Good."

Lucy grabbed him by the tux front and pulled him inside. The body contact had him concentrating on her, on what he would like to do with her and to her.

"Now where's that mike I'm supposed to wear?" she asked.

Thinking about having to wire her without any hanky-panky considering her sister was looking on with interest, Justin gritted his teeth and pulled several items out of his pocket. "Right here."

"Sophisticated stuff," Jenn said.

"I'm a professional," Justin reminded her.

He was nearly as taken aback by her sister's appearance as he was by Lucy's. He would bet Jenn was the spitting image of Kat Ryan in her mid-twenties.

"Can I watch?" Jenn asked with a big grin.

Lucy said, "Why not? All he's going to do is wire me."

That's all he would be able to do, though Justin had visions of his own about what he would *like* to do.

"All right, let's get this thing started," he groused, selecting the tiny mike. "We'll have to tape this in your...'' He waved at the lacings of her bustier. "Here." Palms sweating at the thought of touching Lucy to get the mike in place, he offered it to her, hoping she could manage it on her own. "Can you thread it upward from the waist?"

"If I take a really big breath."

When she did so and started weaving the mike upward, her breasts threatened to spill from the top of the corset, and to keep his mind where it belonged, Justin concentrated on connecting the wire to the transmitter so he could test the system.

"Okay, it's in place," Lucy said a moment later.

"But I can see it." Justin took the wire and wiggled it backward, all the while looking down the front of her corset. Discomfort made him clumsy. "Okay, that's too far down," he muttered.

Silently cursing, he reached in to adjust the mike against her breast. The soft flesh against his fingertips made him light-headed, and he couldn't get his hand out fast enough.

A snicker from behind him made him aware of Jenn's amusement.

"Do we need to tape it in place?" Lucy asked.

"That top is so tight the mike isn't going anywhere. Now I've got to figure out what to do with the transmitter." Though it was compact, so was her outfit. "We need to secure it someplace where it doesn't show. Usually I would put it in back, at your waist, but there's nothing here to hide it."

Jenn said, "She can wear my cape for extra drama and camouflage."

"Good," Justin said, securing the transmitter with a bit less clumsiness.

"Let's just hope it doesn't get too hot at this party," Lucy said. "What about the receiver and recorder?"

Had her voice actually changed or was she doing that husky thing on purpose? Did she even have a clue as to what she was doing to him?

He lifted the rest of the equipment from his other pocket. "I'll be monitoring you personally."

She pointed to the tiny flesh-colored earpiece. "What if someone notices that."

"Hopefully they'll think it's a hearing aid."

"This is starting to sound dangerous," Jenn said, frowning with disapproval, as she handed over the cape.

"We've got it all worked out," Lucy quickly assured her sister.

On some level Jenn had to know they were taking chances but was just registering the fact, Justin thought. He hoped she wasn't going to be too difficult.

"We'll be fine," he said. "Your sister is safe in my hands."

"I'm not too sure about that," Jenn muttered, helping Lucy with the dark purple velvet cape. "But I trust you won't do anything foolish, right?"

Justin and Lucy exchanged glances, and together said, "Right."

"I THINK I'D BETTER LET you off here," Justin said, pulling the car to the curb just down the street from the mansion. "The wrong person might notice we're together."

"Good thinking." Understandably nervous, Lucy took a big breath. "So you think I'll do, right?"

"You do it for me, Luci-i-ille," Justin murmured, leaning over to kiss her.

Lucy knew she ought to protest, ought to stop this before she got too distracted, but she simply couldn't help herself. This could be their last kiss and she couldn't let it go.

Her tongue dueled with Justin's and her head went light. And when she felt his hand on her breast, she felt like abandoning the plan and going home with him to make love.

Justin broke the kiss, his hand still on her breast. "Just checking," he murmured, "to see that the mike is still in place."

Lucy smacked him playfully. "You're just taking advantage now, Mr. Guidry."

"Of course I am. And you object *why?*"

Grinning at him, Lucy wanted to say she had no objections, that he could take advantage of her like this forever, but she couldn't get the words out. Instead, she reached out to rub his lips with her fingertips. And he tried to bite them.

"Stop that. I'm just trying to get rid of the evidence."

"You'd better get going or I won't be able to let you go."

Heart fluttering, wishing it were so, Lucy slipped out of the car and sauntered down the street in her

Goth finery, turning only once to see Justin wave at her before driving off. When she turned again, she almost ran into an older woman, whose eyes opened wide with shock.

"I'm trying on a Halloween costume," Lucy said before heading for the mansion with twelve pillars and three stories.

As instructed, she entered fifteen minutes before the party start time. When she spotted her mother in the foyer, her heart nearly stopped. But while Mama glanced up at the new arrival, she didn't react. Lucy breathed a sigh of relief. Her own mother hadn't recognized her.

Quickly, she found Emile's contact, who guided her to her station in the first floor parlor. It was cleared of everything but a half-dozen small tables with donation bowls for the psychic entertainment, a bar and a food station. Drinks and appetizers would be served by waiters in this room and in the smaller parlor and formal dining room on the other side of the foyer. The sit-down dinner would be hosted in the third-floor ballroom.

Lucy sat down to wait, and to pass the time, practiced laying out her own tarot. She found it hard to concentrate. So much depended on tonight.

And when the night was over...

Soft music filled the air and guests began filtering into the ballroom dressed in their designer finery—women in formal gowns and sparkling jewelry and men in dark tuxes.

Lucy's pulse skipped a beat or two. This was it. Show time.

Thankfully, her first few customers were not handsome, married politicians whose name began with *C*. She relaxed a little, though still keeping an eye out for her prey. Not that he was guaranteed to want his tarot read, but she was the only tarot reader in the room...

She spotted Mama, who was still oblivious to her daughter's presence.

And Daddy, who was not. He passed by and nodded, his signal that he'd done what she'd asked. She glanced around and saw that he had.

After finishing with another customer, she spotted Justin. He was so damn attractive in his rented tux that her pulse triggered and juices started flowing.

Would it always be like this?

Would she always quicken just getting a glimpse of him through a crowd?

"Are you free to read my tarot?" a deep male voice interrupted.

"Yes, of course..." Lucy nearly choked as she looked up into the handsome face of Louisiana senator Carlin Montgomery.

17

WITH HER PULSE gone ragged, Lucy softly choked out, "Sit, please."

Carlin Montgomery was a good-looking man with a winning smile. Winning enough to fool a young girl into falling in love with him? Lucy wondered.

She set down the cards in front of him, saying, "Cut please," then watched his face to see if he reacted to the artwork.

He cut, then said, "Interesting deck," and her heart skipped a beat.

"Yes, I inherited it from a friend—another tarot reader who unfortunately died recently."

Montgomery didn't comment. His face muscles didn't so much as twitch. Lucy couldn't get a read on him, no matter how hard she tried. While she laid out the cards in a Celtic cross pattern, she glanced over Montgomery's shoulder to see that Justin was nearby, very aware of who was at her table.

"So what do you see there?" he asked. "Am I going to win the election?"

"I see that you're very ambitious...and in the recent past, you've done things you want to keep hidden."

He laughed. "All politicians have secrets, Missy."

"But someone knows yours. That person could be dangerous to you."

Montgomery sat back in his seat and frowned at her. "I'm not sure where you're going with this, but I'm not liking it much."

"I'm simply reading the cards."

"The hell you are. I know you supposedly psychic people like to add drama to your readings, but you're just carrying this too far."

With that, a disgusted Montgomery rose, dropped a twenty in the donation bowl, and walked away.

Lucy glanced at Justin. He was keeping an eye on the irritated politician, who took a drink from a roving waiter's tray and then found a woman to charm.

Another customer approached Lucy, so she had to let go of the senator, not knowing if she'd hit a nerve because he was guilty...or because he was simply ticked because he found her outrageous.

The hour passed slowly, even though she read tarot for several more customers before spotting Charles Cahill in the crowd. Dinner would be served in another twenty minutes or so. People were already being herded toward the central staircase to make their way up to the third-floor ballroom. Lucy worried that she would never have a shot at Cahill. But the next thing she knew, Justin was part of the Councilman's group. A moment later, the two men were laughing together and Justin pointed to her.

Cahill nodded and approached her table. "I hear you give the most interesting readings in town. Considering how many psychics New Orleans has, that's saying a lot. So how good are you?''

"One way to find out," she murmured.

"All right then."

Cahill sat and Lucy had him cut the deck. He showed no interest in the artwork, but stared at her, his mouth curved in a slight smile. Lucy wasn't smiling, though. She was getting a goosey feeling from the cards that she didn't like, one that made her uneasy.

She laid out the cards starting with the one he picked, which represented him—the Hierophant. "Well, that's appropriate for a politician in power," she murmured of the figure in ecclesiastic robes, crossing it with a Ten of Swords and the High Priestess. "You're facing much adversity," she said, recognizing that *she* was the source.

As she laid out the rest, her breath caught in her throat. She hadn't set this up. She frowned at the Six of Cups reversed that represented his far past and that spoke to her of things done to him she couldn't have imagined.

"What is it?"

"I'm sorry…someone in your past was very cruel to you…had you under his…no, *her* power.…" It was as if the cards were speaking to her, through her, when she said, "You were in great pain, and you lost everything."

Lucy met Cahill's gaze and saw the truth of what she'd just said in his expression. Someone had done something terrible to him in his youth.

He quickly covered, saying, "So tell me something I don't know."

Lucy looked to the right at his future—Judgment—and said, "You're going to be caught."

"At what?"

She fingered the card to the left that represented the recent past—Death. "Something you've done recently."

"I've done a lot of things, *chère*. You'll have to be more specific."

His unctuous tone sent a chill through Lucy. She blinked at him, then couldn't stop herself from being direct. "A young woman…who disappeared."

The way he was looking at her gave her the creeps. Cahill wasn't offended the way Montgomery had been. More like he was amused.

"And what is it you think I've done with this young woman?"

Lucy got a quick image of a girl on her knees in front of Cahill, whose features were slack with lust. "Things you shouldn't have."

He laughed. "That's pretty broad. Can you narrow it down some?"

"She was too young…underage…" Lucy didn't know where that came from, but the words choked out of her rang true. "…and she threatened you with exposure."

"You have an active imagination."

"Active enough to see a knife." She could, in her mind's eye, something that had never happened to her before. No doubt about it—her sixth sense was telling her that Cahill was definitely the one.

"Ah, now there we are. You think I killed the little twit, don't you?"

The breath caught in her throat. "Did you?"

"No. I don't know what happened to Theresa. I tried telling her sister Erica that, but the bitch was going to bring me up on charges. Not that they would have stuck, but it would have ruined my career. Then that other so-called psychic tried to blackmail me with the knowledge." His voice went soft and threatening when he said, "You know what happened to *her*. And now what is it *you* want, Lucy Ryan?"

Her eyes widened at the mention of Theresa...at his knowing who she was...at the gun he pointed at her from the folds of his jacket so that no one else could see.

"Justice," Lucy croaked. She could feel her pulse in her throat. It pounded hard enough to choke her. And her insides knotted so that she could hardly breathe at all. "Do you plan to kill me here, in front of all these people?"

She darted her gaze to Justin, who swung around toward her. But before he could step off, Kat Ryan stepped in front of him, blocking his path.

"Not here." With the gun barrel still pointed at her, Cahill indicated she should rise. "If you don't want me to shoot someone you care about...let's take a walk."

There was no helping it. She had to obey. Though most of the crowd had advanced up to the formal dinner, too many innocent people were still in the vicinity, including Justin and her mother. She would be all right, she told herself.

Besides, Justin wouldn't let anything happen to her. He'd promised.

A quick glance told here he was trying his best to dance around her mother, but Mama looked distraught and caught on to his arm and wouldn't let go. She danced him around so Justin's back was to Lucy.

"If you're wondering how I recognized you, Lucy Ryan, my man Walter staked out your friend and followed him to that charming little cottage on Magazine where he picked you up."

Lucy felt as if her legs were wooden as Cahill pushed her to the wall, then behind a set of heavy velvet drapes.

He went on. "Not a very competent investigator. Your loss."

A hidden door led outside. Lucy wanted to pull free and call for help, but Cahill opened the door and shoved her through to the garden.

JUSTIN FINALLY pulled free of Lucy's mother and whirled around, seeking out Lucy. She was gone!

"Mr. Guidry, please tell me what's going on!" Kat Ryan cried again.

Her voice reverberated through his head as he ran across the room and frantically looked for an exit. A heavy velvet drapery looked slightly askew and he pulled it from the wall to find a hidden door.

Justin slipped outside onto a small porch to see Cahill down in the garden, pulling something from his pocket. A click and a blade sprang free. A switchblade!

"Cahill!" Justin yelled, vaulting forward over the railing.

The politician's hand wavered and Lucy shoved at him, but before she could get away, Cahill caught her arm and twirled her body into his, yelling, "Take care of him!"

Cahill's two thugs got between Justin and the politician. Justin swung at Mr. Shoe Fetish—the guy they'd identified as Phil Beatty—and made contact with his jaw, but the other one, Walter something, grabbed him from behind. Phil got in a good punch that snapped back his head. But as the thug came at him for more, Justin levered his body against his captor and kicked out with both feet to catch Phil in the gut. Then he dropped forward and toppled Walter over his head.

About to go after Cahill, Justin realized they were surrounded by a half dozen burly men, two wearing tuxes, who were fast tightening the circle. More of Cahill's bodyguards! But rather than looking as if he were in control, the politician seemed ready to panic.

Two of the men stepped over to the ones on the ground, got them flat on their faces and knelt on their backs to hold them there.

"It's over, Cahill," came a familiar voice from behind Justin, just as sirens wailed nearby. "If you want to live, let my daughter go and drop your weapons. Now!"

Even as Jack Ryan came down the stairs, Cahill obeyed and Lucy ran to her father and threw her arms around his neck. "Thank you, Daddy!"

Though Justin wanted in the worst way to wrest her from her father's arms and hold her close forever, he held his ground, waited for her to come to him. He thought Lucy's expression was one of longing as their gazes met, but she didn't budge from her father's side.

As if they meant nothing to each other. Is that how this would all end? Justin wondered sadly.

And then the moment was gone when the sirens stopped yards away. The side gate opened and Lucy's mother came flying around the mansion followed by uniformed police, weapons drawn, Detective Mike Hebert bringing up the rear.

LUCY SAGGED with relief once Cahill and his two thugs were read their rights and carted off. After reassuring her mother that she was just fine and that she would tell her everything later, she asked her father to lead her back into the fund-raiser. The dock workers her father had hired to protect her left, muttering their gratitude that they could finally get out of their tuxes, loosening their bow ties as they practically ran to their cars.

That left her, Justin and Detective Mike Hebert to talk things out.

"Somehow I get the feeling I was left out of the loop a bit," Justin said.

"I asked Daddy to provide us with backup. I didn't want you to get shot again, even if you *are* wearing your bulletproof vest. Daddy employs some of the toughest and most loyal dock workers in the country.''

"But you left me out of the loop *why?*"

"You said I didn't believe in myself. I wanted to prove that you were wrong. Telling Daddy everything, getting him to help was a big step in that direction for me."

"There's a certain twisted logic to that, I suppose." Justin looked at Mike. "And you arrived in the nick of time to make an arrest *why?*"

"Lucky coincidence. Mrs. Ryan led us out here. But we came because our geek retrieved the deleted e-mails on Theresa Vaughn's laptop. Lover boy was using a fake name, but we were able to track his e-mails back to his office account. So we were headed here to arrest Cahill anyway."

"You found proof that he's the murderer?" Lucy asked.

"Proof that he sexually assaulted a minor. Theresa was only seventeen when she fell under his spell. It's the best we could do for the moment. Poor kid, she's undoubtedly another murder victim. We just haven't found her body yet."

"Cahill said he didn't kill her," Lucy said. "That he didn't know what happened to her."

"And you believe him?" Justin asked.

"He admitted to killing both Erica and Sophie, so why would he lie about Theresa?"

"He admitted to murder? Too bad no one else heard it."

"We have it on tape," Justin told him. "Lucy's wired."

"We'll see if we can get it to hold up as evidence," Mike said. "But back to Theresa. If she's not dead, then where?"

Lucy shook her head. "I tried to find her," she said, still wondering why she'd dreamed about the Goth club, instead. Then it hit her. "Wait a minute…maybe I did!"

"Did what?" Mike asked.

"Dreamed her."

"Huh?"

"Don't ask," Justin said. "Just believe her."

Lucy wanted to challenge that, but later. "All this time, she's been hiding in plain sight!"

She borrowed Justin's cell to call Jenn and get the name and address of the Goth club. She made arrangements to meet her sister there. Justin suggested Mike might want to come along. Thankfully, the detective didn't argue the point.

They hurried to their cars.

"I couldn't figure out why I dreamed about Jenn last night," Lucy said when she and Justin were speeding toward the club, Mike following in his unmarked car. "She was arguing with another Goth. I told her about it, and she said it was this girl Tess who ran away because she was in trouble. Jenn was trying to convince her to return to her parents who loved her, to let them help her. I simply didn't put it together until now."

"You mean Tess—"

"Is Theresa Vaughn."

Jenn was waiting for them at the door of the club. And Tess/Theresa was inside.

At first the girl-in-disguise denied ever hearing of Theresa Vaughn, but when Lucy told her she'd seen Sophie killed by Charles Cahill and that Sophie had been looking for her with her sister Erica, Theresa broke down in tears and admitted all. She'd threatened to go to Cahill's wife and tell her about their affair. Then Cahill had threatened her. She'd been terrified for her own life and had been living first on the street and then with a couple of Goths ever since.

Lucy introduced Theresa to Justin and to Mike, who volunteered to take her home to her father. Though she was crying and still terrified, Theresa agreed.

After thanking Jenn, Lucy left with Justin. She was filled with a happiness that made her eyes sting.

"This whole last week was so horrible, but something good came of it. We did get Cahill before he could kill again. And Mrs. Vaughn can come home now," she said, remembering Mr. Vaughn saying she couldn't bear the loss of both daughters. "Theresa will need her."

"We're some team," Justin said as they reached the car.

"Investigating."

"In every way." He took her arm and turned her against the car door. "We're good together, Lucy Ryan. I think we should think about a more permanent arrangement."

He was so close he made her body want to scream

yes. But more than bodies were involved here. "You and me?" she murmured. "Not hardly."

Justin rested a hand on the car behind her and leaned in closer. "Are you saying you don't care for me?"

"I love you, Justin, so much it hurts, because sometimes love isn't enough."

"What more do you need?"

"You asked me to believe in myself when you didn't believe in me."

"Who says?"

"*You* said."

"Uh-uh. I said I didn't know what to believe when it came to your dreams."

"Exactly."

"But I did give that dream credence, *chère*. Why do you think I was wearing the bulletproof vest when I was shot?"

Lucy blinked at that. "Because of me? You're saying you believed me?"

"I believed *you* believed in the dream, and that's what matters, because I believe in *you*. Besides, I'm a man who likes to hedge my bets. Right now, I would bet you want me to kiss you."

He did and Lucy nearly melted. Heart fluttering with an outpouring of emotion, she pushed him away. "You'd lose that bet. I want a whole lot more than a simple kiss."

HE GAVE IT TO HER.

Upon entering his loft, Justin kissed her again, his hands stripping her of her clothes. Anxious to feel skin-on-skin, she tore at his, too.

Then they were both naked.

He leaned her back against the sofa, spread her thighs and knelt between them. She was breathing heavily before his tongue even slid along her soft inner flesh, opening it to his rhythmic stroking. With love in her heart she watched his head between her thighs. She tangled her fingers in his dark hair and opened herself wider, allowing him deeper access.

It was a dream, the whole thing. She was too happy for this to be real.

He made a hot sound and fluid flowed from her to meet his tongue. He lapped at her like he couldn't get enough of her until she felt ready to burst with joy.

Then he tested her with a finger, never stopping the titillation of his tongue, and she knew what was coming. She could trust in dreams.

She closed her eyes and arched her back.

His fingers were inside her now. One…two…she couldn't take more even though she wanted it. She would take all of him inside herself if she could.

She spread wider…arched higher…fists tightening in his hair as she tried to hold on. But the intensity of her response as he stroked her was too great to ignore.

Letting herself go, she cried out, and before the sound completed, he was swallowing her, kissing her. And then he was inside her, fulfilling what she needed most…to be one with him.

She reached between them and stroked him with her fingertips, excited again when she felt her slippery fluids on his shaft.

"Luci-i-ille," he moaned.

"That's my name…don't wear it out," she whispered, wrapping her arms around his neck and her legs around his thighs, and gave him a ride that he could dream about when they came together and tumbled down onto the weathered leather.

Lucy couldn't think of a thing she wanted more at this moment than to sleep safely in Justin's arms.…

THEY JOINED as one in the sweet-smelling garden where they'd made love the night he'd proposed. Her heart thundered as he kissed her with love and promise.

Applause reminded her that they weren't alone and her cheeks filled with heat as she looked around at the audience, her gaze stopping at her sister who was wearing a stunning lavender gown.

She smelled her bouquet of gardenias before pitching it—her sister caught it and appeared either surprised or horrified, she wasn't sure which.

Grinning, she turned back into the arms of the man she would always love and who had promised to love her in return.

Her husband.

e♦HARLEQUIN.com

The Ultimate Destination for Women's Fiction

For **FREE online reading**, visit www.eHarlequin.com now and enjoy:

Online Reads
Read **Daily** and **Weekly** chapters from our Internet-exclusive stories by your favorite authors.

Interactive Novels
Cast your vote to help decide how these stories unfold...then stay tuned!

Quick Reads
For shorter romantic reads, try our collection of Poems, Toasts, & More!

Online Read Library
Miss one of our online reads? Come here to catch up!

Reading Groups
Discuss, share and rave with other community members!

For great reading online, visit www.eHarlequin.com today!

HARLEQUIN *Blaze*™

Cover Model Contest Update

We asked you to send us pictures of your hot, gorgeous *and* romantic guys, and you did!

From all of the entries, we finally selected the winner and put him right where he deserves to be: on one of our covers.

Check him out on the front of

VERY TRULY SEXY

by Dawn Atkins

Harlequin Blaze #155
October 2004

Don't miss this story that's every bit as hot and romantic as the guy on the cover!

Look for this book at your favorite retail outlet.